COME AND HAVE A GO IF YOU THINK YOU'RE SMART ENOUGH!

Are you **SMART** enough to collect the series?

COME AND HAVE A GO IF YOU THINK YOU'RE SMART ENOUGH!

COME AND HAVE A GO IF YOU THINK YOU'RE COOL ENOUGH!

COME AND HAVE A GO IF YOU THINK YOU'RE MAD ENOUGH!

COME AND HAVE A GO IF YOU THINK YOU'RE RICH ENOUGH!

connor mcleod is blind

COME AND HAVE A GO IF YOU THINK YOU'RE SMART ENOUGH!

Haydn Middleton

Hippo

Scholastic Children's Books,
Commonwealth House, 1–19 New Oxford Street,
London, WC1A 1NU, UK
a division of Scholastic Ltd
London ~ New York ~ Toronto ~ Sydney ~ Auckland
Mexico City ~ New Delhi ~ Hong Kong

First published in the UK by Scholastic Ltd, 1999

Text copyright © Haydn Middleton, 1999
Illustrations copyright © Philip Reeve, 1999

ISBN 0 439 01080 2

All rights reserved

Typeset by DP Photosetting, Aylesbury, Bucks
Printed and bound by Bath Press, Bath

1 2 3 4 5 6 7 8 9 10

The rights of Haydn Middleton and Philip Reeve to be
identified respectively as the author and illustrator of this work have
been asserted by them in accordance with the Copyright,
Designs and Patents Act, 1988.

For Luke and Ed – It's not your fault you were born near the Manor!

Luke Green was so excited, he could hardly stop smiling. It was Boxing Day lunchtime and he kept on checking his brand-new watch. There was less than an hour to go now. And still his mum didn't know a thing about it.

"I don't know why you keep grinning," she said. She was putting plates of cold turkey on the table and having one of her headaches. "You're not going to get any more Christmas presents, you know."

"I know, Mum," Luke replied sweetly. "But it's the season of goodwill to all men, isn't it?" He grinned even wider. "And to all women of course."

"Maybe you'd like to come for a walk with us this afternoon, Luke," said Rodney, his stepdad, as they tucked in. "We could take your binoculars and do a bit of bird-spotting. If we're lucky we might see some jackdaws."

"Sorry, Rodney," Luke answered quickly. "I'm going round to Ian Boulter's house so that we can work together on our geography project."

"On *Boxing* Day?" gasped Mum. "You are keen."

"And I'm very glad to hear it," said Rodney, nodding his head. "It shows that you've got your priorities right. If you work hard now, you can have all the fun you like later. You're a changed boy, Luke."

"And you know why, don't you?" put in his mum. "It's all because you finally agreed with me, and stopped supporting that ridiculous football team."

Luke's toes curled up inside his trainers and he clenched his knife and fork very hard. *Don't call them ridiculous!* He wanted to scream. *They're gods in blue-and-white hoops!* But he couldn't afford to make any mistakes at this late stage. "Yes, Mum," he said meekly.

Mum pulled a face. She hated everything about football from Jimmy Hill's chin to Gary Lineker's adverts for crisps. "I think they must be playing this afternoon," she said, starting to work herself up. "I've already seen some of the half-wits in their hats and scarves walking past. My goodness, they must be dim. I mean, what do they *do* inside that ground for two hours before the game starts? Throw bottles at each other? Stuff themselves with those ghastly-burgers? Stare

2

at the pictures in the programme – because they surely can't *read*?"

"There, there, dear," Rodney calmed her. "Luke knows your views on the world of ... football." He shot her a nervous look, as if she might turn on *him* just for saying the word. "He doesn't need to be reminded."

"Absolutely," said Luke, gobbling up the last of his lunch and taking another glance at his watch. "And now, if you don't mind, I'm itching to get down to that geography project with Ian. It's all about Egypt. Can I go now, please?"

"Ah, Egypt," Rodney began, with a dreamy look on his face. "Plenty of marvellous birds in Egypt. The scarlet ibis, for example..."

"Umm," Luke had to cut in – once Rodney got going on birds, there could be no stopping him. "I said to Ian I'd be there by now. Please can I go?"

"All right then," said his mum. "The Boulters don't live far away, do they? But be back before it gets too dark."

Three minutes later Luke was powering up the hill on his mountain bike. It was brilliantly sunny outside, with just a trace of snow still on the ground. The fans on their way to the Ash Acre stadium walked on the road as well as on both pavements, so Luke had to weave his way around them. Some were singing even before the floodlights rose into view on their massive pylons:

"Castle Al-bee-yon! Castle Al-bee-yon!
We'll Support You Evermore!"

Luke felt his pulse race, his heart pound, and the hairs on the back of his neck stand up. *This* was what life was all about. As far as he was concerned, the only real season of goodwill was the football season.

Turning right on to the main road at the top of the hill, the stream of supporters became a flood. Luke had to get off his bike and wheel it the rest of the way. But not to Ian Boulter's house.

Luke was a strong cyclist but even he couldn't pedal to Belgium and back before dark. Because that was where the Boulter family had moved to, six weeks before. Luke had told a little blue-and-white-hooped lie about the geography project – and since his mum was too snooty to mix with any other kids' parents, she was never going to find out.

Of course, Luke didn't like lying. Especially about football. But if his mum insisted on being so horrible to him about his beloved club, then there really was no other way. Especially today – because this was going to be the proudest day of Luke Green's entire football-loving life.

2

CASTLE ALBION FC

Founded 1872

---

said the huge blue letters over the front
entrance up ahead. But before Luke got there,
he turned into the club's official car park and
bent down to lock his bike.

"Hey, sonny!" shouted a steward in a bright
yellow coat. "You can't leave that there."

"Oh yes I can," beamed Luke, straightening
up and pulling his binoculars out of his saddle-
bag. (He *would* soon be watching some
brightly-coloured creatures on the wing – but
they would be wearing Adidas boots and be
covered in sponsors' logos.)

"Can't you read? This car park is for players
and officials only."

"But I am one."

"Oh yeah, Mr Clever. One what? Player or official?"

"Well *both* – in a way." Luke reached across and plucked the glossy match programme out of the steward's pocket. Before the man could say David Batty, Luke flicked to the inside back page and pointed at the little blurry photo. Yes!

TODAY'S MATCH MASCOT: Luke Green of 91, Cranham Hill, a loyal supporter of the Albion since the age of seven. He likes computer games and all kinds of music except boy bands. His favourite Albion player is Ruel Bibbo and his ambition is to see Albion rise to Division Two of the Nationwide League – or else win the FA Cup!

"OK then?" Luke grinned, handing back the programme before striding down to the club offices. Out of Ash Acre came loud waves of singing. The ancient tannoy system was crackling away as usual with messages that no one could understand. The fried-onion stink of the ghastly-burgers was enough to make even the toughest fan's head spin. There was *such* a spring to Luke's step.

Match Day Mascot! For the Nationwide Division Three game against Carlisle United. And he had organized every bit of it himself. Paid the fee from his own saved-up pocket money. Sent in a copy of his latest school photo. That steward was right. He *was* Mr Clever. As smart as a Paul Merson through-ball. He rubbed his hands and chanted under his breath with all the others:

"Castle Al-bee-yon! Castle Al-bee-yon! We'll Support You Evermore!"

But once inside, he came down to earth with a bump. A woman in a club blazer dropped a pile of kit into his arms. Then another woman told him to go and get changed in the toilet. And when he came out, still wearing his trainers because he owned no boots, no one could tell him what to do with his street clothes and binoculars. Everyone was tearing about like mad, and smiling at him kindly, but Luke didn't recognize any of the faces. And down here under the main stand, the noise of the crowd sounded weird – like the buzz of a very large and angry bee.

Luke looked at his watch. Two forty-five. Kick-off in fifteen minutes. He was supposed to have been taken to the changing rooms by now. Shaken hands with all the players. But he hadn't even *seen* a player yet. Then there was the tour of the trophy room. Not that he would need very long for that. There was only one cup in there – for winning the old Fourth Division, twenty years before Luke was born.

He sighed but he wasn't too surprised. That

was Castle Albion for you. It was a friendly little club but pretty disorganized, both off and on the pitch. According to Luke's real dad, it had always been that way – even in ancient times.

Apparently, once when *he* was a boy, he had bought a ticket for a big cup-tie against Aston Villa. But the club had sold the ticket for his seat twice over, so Luke's dad never got to see the game. Just typical.

With his clothes in his arms, Luke wandered away from the offices and lounges. Finding himself in a narrow, peeling corridor, he nudged back a fire-door. As soon as the door clicked shut behind him, an eerie silence fell. Then at once it was broken by a man's roar. It came from behind a scuffed blue door directly in front of Luke. Home Team, it said – the Castle Albion dressing room! And as Luke stepped closer, he realized that the roar was coming from manager Benny Webb, giving his pre-match team talk.

"Football is a beautiful, *beautiful* game!" Big Benny was yelling. "If you play it the way it should be played – the way I am always *telling* you to play it – then it's the most beautiful thing in the *world.* But you've got to be *organized...*" His voice suddenly sank to no more than a whisper. Luke had to press his ear to the door. "...and that means using your *brains*, right...?" His voice went lower still. Luke pressed his ear even harder. "*Think* your way past the opposition. Catch them out with the element of..." Just as his voice almost disappeared, he exploded into the last word: "*SURPRISE!*" – which made Luke jump so much that he jerked his shoulder against the door, knocked it back, and fell forward in a heap on to the dressing-room floor.

3

The next ten minutes were a bit of a blur. The club had forgotten all about the matchday mascot. And there was no time now for Benny Webb to introduce Luke to all the players. The next thing he knew, he was being hauled to his feet. One of the subs took his clothes and put a brand-new ball in his hands. Then he was hustled out and was leading his team up the long dark tunnel!

As the din of the crowd turned from a bee-hum into the bellowing of 3,165 mad bulls, Luke felt the hand of Albion's skipper, Stuart "Gaffer" Mann, squeeze his shoulder. That gave him all the confidence he needed. He raced out into the crisp sunlight, grinning fit to burst, and hoofed the ball high up into the air.

"Blimey," laughed the skipper behind him. "I've never seen a kid hit it *that* far before." And that was just the beginning.

Luke knew he didn't have long. The mascots only got a few minutes to pass the ball around among the players, and maybe take a shot or two at eighteen-year-old "Madman" Mort in goal. Then they stood around watching the captains toss-up, shook hands with anyone with a hand to shake – and that was pretty well it.

"Today's Albion mascot is Luke Green!" blared the tannoy. Or rather: "*To-crack Al-pop buzz-buzz ug Loo Gee!*" Luke didn't care about that. He had dashed over to the penalty area and started passing the ball back and forth to his hero, Ruel Bibbo. "You're doing all right, kid," Ruel yelled, and after passing it, each of them jogged a few steps further back to receive the return.

Ruel was a veteran striker. Ages ago he had been one of the first black footballers to play for England. After years and years at West Brom, Chelsea and Tottenham he was ending his career at Castle Albion. And even though he was older than Luke's dad, and twenty times as injury prone, he was still different class. By now he had back-pedalled to the far post, and Luke was out near the touchline. "Stick it on me head then, son!" Ruel called. It was a good job he pointed at his forehead – the chants of the crowd drowned out what he said.

The ball came rolling back Luke's way, and without trapping it first, he sent in a hard, right-foot cross. It was exactly the height he knew

Ruel liked it. He just had to flick his neck and the ball arrowed past Madman into the net.

"Bet you can't do that again," shouted Madman, rolling out another ball towards the touchline. Luke stepped forward and whipped in another deadly accurate cross. Ruel had it for breakfast. Two-nil.

"Do it again and I'll give you a big sloppy kiss," Madman said. It was easy to see where the big guy got his nickname from. Out came another ball, in went another inch-perfect cross, and Ruel Bibbo grabbed a pre-match hat-trick.

Thankfully Madman just shook his head. But the striker waved at Luke to come across into the penalty area. "That's the best service I've had since I played with Chris Waddle," he beamed, clapping Luke on the back. "And he could only ever cross it properly in training. What are *you* like in matches, son?"

Before Luke could answer, the ref blew his whistle for the captains to toss for ends. Luke had to trot across and start all the hand-shaking. Gaffer Mann called heads and lost. He wrinkled up his nose at Luke. "Should have let you do it, shouldn't I?" he said. "If your tossing-up's anything like your kicking. Off you go then, mate. Your togs are in the dug-out."

Luke jogged back towards the main stand. He raised a hand when the home fans there clapped him politely. Then some Carlisle fans behind the Town End goal directed a quick chant at him. The words were so rude that if his mum had heard them, her hair would have turned back to its proper colour. Luke laughed.

"Come on then, lad," said Benny Webb, holding Luke's jeans, shirt, fleece and binoculars. "You get to keep the kit, and your seat's up there behind the dug-out." A great roar went up as the match began. But the manager, in his huge sheepskin coat, kept looking at Luke, a thoughtful expression on his bearded face. "Look son, we messed up on your big day earlier. If you get yourself around here at ten o'clock on Thursday morning, you can meet all the players at training. You'll still be on your school holidays, right?"

"Yeah, I will," said Luke eagerly.

"And bring your boots next time," said Benny. "You can have a run-out with the lads. I liked the way you were putting those crosses in. I'm telling you son, if our lot could find Ruel's head like that, we'd score ten every game."

"Thanks, Mr Webb," gasped Luke. But Benny had already turned away to watch the game. "*Think* about it, Albion!" he was roaring in a mixture of fury and pain. "Oh, use your brains! Be *SMART*!"

Luke enjoyed the game but Albion weren't at their best. Through the binoculars, he could

13

clearly see the look of frustration on Ruel's face. Left full-back Craig Edwards got forward to scramble a goal just after half-time, then Madman was beaten by a soft long-range effort and the match ended one-one. That left Albion sixteenth in the division. It was starting to look as if promotion was out of the question for yet another year. But at least there was the FA Cup Third Round to look forward to on the eighth of January.

Just like in Luke's dad's day, Albion had been drawn against Aston Villa at home. And it was going to be televised live! That would be a cracker. But so would the training session on Thursday morning. *Training session!* With the Albion! It was getting better and better.

After the game, Luke changed back into his ordinary clothes then went for a coke and a cake in a café. It was getting dark, but he didn't want to arrive home while the football crowd were still rolling down the hill. That might make his mum suspicious. When at last he did get back, he left his new kit and binoculars in his saddlebag and went into the kitchen with a big smile.

"Useful afternoon's work?" asked his mum.

"Brilliant," Luke replied. "We're going to have another good crack at it on Thursday morning. I said I'd go round at about ten."

Thursday turned out to be a bit tricky. Luke's mum gave him a list of stuff to buy at the shops near Ian Boulter's house. And she said she wanted him back by twelve o'clock sharp for an early lunch. Her favourite gardening programme was on the TV at twenty-past and she wasn't going to miss it for anyone.

Luke tore around the shops first. And because the bag was too big to leave in his saddle-bag, he took it to the Albion changing rooms. This time the door was open, so he didn't have to crash in head first. "Ooh, look who's been shopping then," cried Madman Mort. "You haven't got a brand-new central midfielder in there, have you?"

"Or a goalie who doesn't think Save of the Season means you only have to stop one shot a year," snarled Narris Phiz, who played in central midfield for Albion and – just once – for his home country of Trinidad.

Then Saturday's scorer, Craig Edwards,

snatched the pineapple out of the top of the bag. With a cry of "Head it!" he hurled the fruit at rookie winger Chrissie Pick. But the YTS lad – sitting and combing his huge Brylcreemed plume of golden hair in a hand-mirror – managed to duck. The spiky fruit smashed into the bottom of Carl Davey, who had just finished changing and was bending over to adjust his socks. What Carl screamed then was bluer than the hoops on Albion's shirts.

"Lads, lads," shouted Benny Webb, above all the laughs and threats. "Our mascot here has come back to meet you lot, although after Saturday's display I can't see why he still wants to. So I thought I'd let him join in training. If you watch 'im closely, you might pick up a few tips." Amid more catcalls he bent down to pick up the pineapple and handed it to Luke, wrinkling up his nose.

During the next hour and a half, Luke had to keep pinching himself. Not because he couldn't believe that he was training with the mighty Albion's first-team squad. But because it was so much like being at school. The players were just like a bunch of kids. In fact, Benny Webb had to yell at them far more often than Mr Riley, Luke's PT teacher, ever had to yell at his class.

While they ran laps of the pitch, half a dozen of them were playing their own game of tag. When

Benny tried to organize a piggy-back race, a massive chicken-fight broke out. And in a penalty-taking session, Madman Mort kept on putting off the kickers by pulling up his tracksuit top to reveal a latex, white-on-black skeleton chest.

"And you thought Gazza was daft, didn't you, son?" Benny sighed at Luke. "But you've done pretty good yourself, even if you haven't brought your boots again. You're in good shape for a little 'un, I'll give you that. How about playing in the practice game now?"

Luke didn't have to be asked twice. It was a ten-a-side game for the nineteen-man squad with Benny himself making up the numbers. Luke had hoped to link up with Ruel Bibbo, but the big guy had strained his groin taking a penalty and limped off to the treatment room.

"The physio gets lonely if he don't see Ruel every half hour," sneered Chopper Foggon, the central-defensive hard man with muscles in places where most people don't have places. "Keeps him in work, he does."

Luke was told to play on the right side of midfield. "Like David Beckham, you know?" said his team captain, Gaffer Mann. "You look a bit like him. Let's see if you can manage to stay on the pitch and play like him."

"OK," said Luke, and with his first touch, he did exactly that. The ball broke to him just inside his own half. Looking up, he noticed that Madman was on the edge of his penalty area, fiddling with his skeleton chest. Luke teed himself up, then launched the ball in a huge, high arc, right over the hopelessly back-pedalling keeper's head and into the net – exactly the way Beckham had scored against Wimbledon on the first day of the 1996–7 season.

Every single person in Ash Acre looked on open-mouthed, first at the ball nestling in the back of the net, then at Luke Green, then back again at the ball.

"He cheated, Boss," shouted Madman, in a tangled heap around the foot of his goalpost, "He's not wearing boots. Anyone can do that in *trainers*!"

That broke the ice. Just about every one of the other players ran up and formed a queue to shake hands with the goalscorer. Young Chrissie Pick and midfielder Michael "Half-Fat" Milkes went down on both knees and said, "We are not worthy!"

"There you go, son," nodded Benny Webb, the last to congratulate him with a firm shake of the hand. "You thought you'd come here to meet this mob. Now they've come to meet you." He turned to the others. "You see what I mean: the element of *surprise*? This kid plays *smart* football."

The game went on. Each time Luke took posses-sion, he played the ball simply and accurately.

No frills, no tricks. From one of his passes Gaffer Mann tapped in a second goal. But as Luke jogged back for the restart, he glanced up at the stadium clock and saw that it was eleven-fifty. He had to be home in ten minutes!

"Sorry, Mr Webb," he called out, racing for the dressing room. "Thanks for everything but I've got to be back by twelve."

"Why's that?" asked right full-back Dennis Meldrum. "Frightened you'll turn into a pumpkin?"

"Or a pineapple," said Carl Davey, rubbing his bottom.

Luke got changed lightning quick. But when he rushed out of the changing room clutching his bag of goodies, Benny Webb had come off the pitch and was standing waiting at the end of the tunnel. "Come up here a sec, son," he said. Luke went, but the clock was now showing eleven fifty-four. "I'm impressed," Benny said. "Very impressed. That's an educated right foot you've got there."

"Thanks Mr Webb. It was a fantastic morning. But I really do have to go now."

Just then a gob of bird-mess splattered down on the concrete between them. Luke looked up and saw – high in the scrappy old tin roof of the main stand – a nest with some small, long-tailed birds fluttering and chirruping around it.

"Apparently they're black redstarts," Benny Webb told him, stroking his beard. "Over from France for the winter. Other clubs get David Ginola or Patrick Vieira – we got them." He smiled. "Free transfers, though."

Luke backed away down the tunnel. "Cheers then, Mr Webb," he called.

The manager could only stare after him – before jerking his head back to avoid another dollop of bird mess.

5

Friday was the last day of the school holiday. Wanting to make the most of it, Luke went for a bike ride. In the park at the edge of town there was a fantastically steep hill without speed bumps, so Luke spent the afternoon doing wheelies with some of the kids from around there. When it started to get dark he set off for home, but near the park gates he spotted one of his best mates.

"All right, Frederick?" Luke called across, braking hard.

The kid in the big kagoul with the hood up didn't seem to hear. He was juggling a football on his foot, knee, shoulder and neck, while also moving smoothly in time to the music on his Walkman. But then, as Luke dismounted and propped up his bike against a bench, he casually rolled the ball across the grass to him. That was as close as Cool Frederick ever came to saying hello.

Luke stroked the ball back and soon they got

into a regular passing rhythm. "How's it going, then?" Luke asked him when they moved on to heading it to each another.

"Cool," said Frederick after a pause for thought. Luke smiled – as if it could ever be anything else.

Cool Frederick was fifteen days older than him but at times it seemed like fifteen years. Even in the infants, Frederick Dulac had been impossibly cool. His name-tags had been orange like Levi labels, and printed in the same typeface. He had probably worn Calvin Klein nappies as a baby and been born with shades on. But with Cool Frederick, it wasn't just a clothes thing. Even in home-made jeans and a puffer jacket he would have looked sorted.

"Saw you at the Albion on Monday," he said to Luke after a while. "Hey Mascot Man, respect."

That was how cool Frederick was. Unlike all the glory supporters at school who said they loved Man U or Liverpool or Real Madrid, Cool Frederick had been an Albion fan since he was six and *still* no one gave him any stick.

"I went back yesterday as well," Luke told him. "Training with the first team."

"Safe."

"Benny Webb said I had an educated right foot."

"Way to go. You gonna sign for them then? Schoolboy terms?"

"How could I – even if they asked me? I'd need a parent's permission."

"Your mum?" Cool Frederick frowned. "Bad deal, man."

"She's getting worse than ever. When the paper comes now, she rips out all the football pages and throws them away before she starts to read the rest. And she wouldn't buy me any XTR V-brakes for Christmas just because the bloke in the bike-shop looks so much like John Motson. I'd hate to think what would happen if she even *saw* Benny Webb – she hates beards too, you see."

"And Birdman Rodney's no use to you?"

Luke shook his head sadly. Sometimes he wondered if Rodney really hated football *quite* so much as his mum. The other morning he had caught him trying to read the screwed-up bits of newspaper in the pedal-bin as he threw away the tea bags. But he was never going to take Luke's side against his mum. He was way too scared of her himself.

They went back to kicking the ball – left foot, right foot – looping it up softly with the speed taken off, and never once letting it touch the ground. "What about your real dad, though?" asked Cool Frederick. "The guitar man. He's a dude."

"A dude?" grinned Luke. "Right. But I never know when I'm going to see him. He has to travel to wherever he can get gigs, so he can never say when he'll be in town. And anyway, if *he* gave me permission and Mum found out, she'd go ballistic."

"Bummer."

Bummer indeed, thought Luke, who chipped up a pass just as his mate's mobile phone went off. Cool Frederick twisted around, tossed back his head and neatly caught the ball in his fur-trimmed hood. "Ace in the hole!" he purred before whipping out the phone from his pocket and nodding goodbye to Luke, who grinned, went to fetch his bike and continued on his way back home.

When he turned into his street there was an unfamiliar car outside the house. A big but shabby-looking Volvo. As he coasted closer, Luke saw a *Honk if you support the Albion!* sticker on its rear window.

Something weird happened inside Luke's chest. His heart seemed to leap and sink all at the same time. And then, glancing over the bare hedge outside his house, he saw the awful truth.

It was quite dark now, and the visitor had mistakenly gone up the drive, which only led to the back door. Now he was back-tracking, and scrunching along the narrower path of loose chippings that led around to the front. He was about three steps away from the knocker. And he was Benny Webb.

"Pssst! No! *Please*, no!" Luke hissed through the hedge, crouching down in the hope that his mum wouldn't spot him through the window.

Benny turned but at first he couldn't see where the noise was coming from. He put a finger in his ear, waggled it about, then took another step closer to the front door.

"*Mister Webb!* Don't do it. *Please* don't touch that knocker or I'm dead meat!"

Benny swung round fast this time. Fast for him, anyway.

"Here!" Luke pleaded. "I'm here behind the hedge. Oh, come out, Mr Webb. Believe me, you don't want to try talking to anyone inside there."

Benny's eyes narrowed. "Luke? Luke, is that you?" Then thankfully he started coming back down the path, and out again into the street. "Are you all right there, son?" he asked, peering down at the curled-up boy.

"Ssh! Ssh! They'll hear you. Look, drive on up

the hill a bit. There's a left turn, with an off-license and a video shop on the right. I'll talk to you there."

Benny looked puzzled, but got into his car and did as Luke asked. Two minutes later Luke pulled up alongside him on his bike.

"I'm sorry about that, Mr Webb," Luke panted, when Benny managed to wind down his window after it had stuck a couple of times. "It's better like this, though. My mum hates absolutely everything to do with football."

"She's not a fan?"

"The complete and utter opposite. She's like an anti-fan. A fan backwards." Luke thought about that for a moment. "She's a NAF."

"So she wouldn't be keen on you signing associate schoolboy forms with the Albion?" asked Benny, picking up a wad of papers from the passenger seat and waving them. Luke saw there was a splodge of black redstart mess on the shoulder of his sheepskin coat. "I like what I've seen of you, son. I like the way you play and I like your attitude. You've got a natural football brain. And you don't get many of them for five quid nowadays. Not for five million neither. But my hands are tied if your mum says no."

"I'm really sorry, Mr Webb."

"Oh, forget about the Mr Webb. Everyone calls me Boss and I call everyone son. All right?" He tossed the forms back on to the passenger seat.

"All right then, Boss."

Then Benny looked up at Luke with big sad eyes. "Just tell me this, son – and be straight with me. Your mum's not wanting you to go to Newcastle or Leeds or one of them Premiership clubs with money to burn, is she?"

"No Boss, honestly. She won't even let me play football at school. I told you, she's got this thing about the whole game. She calls it 'trash culture'. It doesn't make sense to her. She can't see why it's like life and death to half the world."

Benny Webb nodded and stroked his beard. "Well, we're not in the money at Castle Albion, son. We're so poor we can hardly pay attention. But if you joined us, we'd make sure you played the game the way it *should* be played."

"I know that, Boss. And I'd love to come to Albion." Luke shrugged. "But really, it's not on. I just can't see a way."

"Oi!" came a shout from one of the shop doorways. "You there, on the bike!" Luke turned to see the man from the off-licence, with his hands on his hips and looking stroppy as usual. "Is that bloke in the car annoying you, sonny?"

"No, no, it's all right," Benny said, craning his neck around Luke. "We're just talking about football."

"Well now, if it isn't the Big Boss himself!" the off-licence man snorted. "*Talking* about football is about all you're good at. Why don't you find someone who can put a decent cross in? And you'd better make that lot of yours pull their fingers out tomorrow afternoon, 'cos if we don't win soon we're gonna go right down to the Football Conference."

Benny smiled. He looked used to being shouted at by complete strangers. "I'd best be off," he said to Luke. "Are you coming to watch tomorrow, son? Southend. They're riding high at the moment. Tough one for us."

"I'll try to be there," said Luke, wondering what excuse he could give his mum this time; *three* geography project sessions in a week was really pushing it. "Thanks for coming round, Boss. Good luck against Southend. And on Tuesday night too – you ought to get a result at Hartlepool."

"The way we're playing, son, we wouldn't get a result in a paddling pool."

As Benny drove off, four girls outside the video shop got into a line, then began to bounce about and sing:

"You're Goin' To The Con-ference,
You're Goin' To The Con-ference,
La-la La Laa, La-la La Laa..."

When Luke got home, he put away his bike and

saw Rodney tinkering with one of his bird tables in the back garden. Luke wanted to tell him about the black redstarts, but that would mean admitting he'd been at the football ground. It was all so pointlessly complicated.

"Ah, Luke," Rodney called over. "Your dad's been on the phone. He's doing a show at the Four Horseshoes tomorrow – a private New Year's Eve party."

"Brilliant! And he wants me to go?"

"Well, that *was* what he wanted – yes." Rodney's already long face went longer behind his glasses. "But your mum wasn't happy about you being in that pub – not during opening hours, anyway. A den of iniquity, she called it. So she said you could go and see your dad there for a couple of hours when it's shut. While he's doing his soundcheck tomorrow afternoon."

"What time in the afternoon?"

"About three. You weren't doing anything, were you?"

Luke looked back blankly. He could have laughed, he could have cried. Castle Albion versus high-flying Southend United was a three o'clock kick-off.

7

Luke arrived at the Four Horseshoes at twenty to three. It was a long ride across town, and he had passed all the Albion fans coming the opposite way. There were a lot from Southend too, in their royal blue. It was a dark, chilly afternoon and the rain lashed down. Luke wasn't feeling too optimistic. Wet conditions didn't usually favour the Albion's style of play. But then again, they tended to wilt in the heat. A thick fog might have suited them best.

He found his dad in the upstairs function-room, sitting on the edge of the small stage. He was twiddling with an amplifier, then striking chords on his electric guitar and trying to get the balance right. The way Luke heard it, he still had a pretty long way to go.

After playing in bands for donkey's years, his dad was now a solo performer. He called himself simply Green. (It had actually been Simply Green for a while.) Some of his bands' names had been bizarre. In his first hippy phase there was Grass Green and the Flowerbeds, followed by Lawn Green and the Herbaceous Borders. Then in the Eighties he briefly fronted Green Means Go – their one and only single, "Little Flashing Man", peaking at number 146 in the charts. Or so he said. Then he'd tried a radical new direction: The Chemical Brothers Grimm was an attempt to mix dance music with spoken fairytales. But that hadn't worked out happily ever after, so now he'd gone back to being a hippie again – ponytail, floral trousers, psychedelic van, the lot – and still he hadn't had a record deal in fifteen years.

"Dad," smiled Luke, crossing the functions room floor to him. It didn't take long to cross it. It was a very small room.

His dad put down his guitar, stood up and hugged him hard. "Great to see you, kid. How's it hangin'?"

"Fine. What are you playing tonight? All the old Flower Power stuff?"

"Yeah. Right on. I've worked up a new seventeen-minute version of the Beatles' "All You Need Is Love". I think that'll go down well with this crowd. You'd hardly recognize it from the original."

No, I bet you wouldn't, thought Luke, glancing at the watch his dad had given him for Christmas. Fifteen minutes to kick-off. "Look, Dad, do you have any idea how long you're going to be in town this time? Only I was hoping to watch the Albion game this afternoon..."

"Say no more. Say no *more*!" He held up his hand. "I'm off again tomorrow but I'll be back on Monday for another gig around here on Tuesday. I've got a bed-and-breakfast room upstairs. I can just as easily see you then, no sweat. I'd come with you to Ash Acre if I didn't have this flippin' soundcheck," his eyes twinkled, "and as long as they hadn't sold the seat twice over."

"Oh cheers, Dad." Luke hugged him again. "Look, I've got to rush, but we'll talk on Monday, right? Late afternoon, after chess club? There's a lot I want to tell you. Have a good gig." He closed his eyes, then through gritted teeth he said what he knew his dad needed to hear: "Sock it to 'em, baby!"

The lights were all against Luke as he rode back across town. The rain was teeming down harder than ever too. While he was locking his bike he could tell from the crowd's noise that the game had started. He didn't have enough money to pay for a seat so he ran round to stand at the West End, wishing he'd worn a more rainproof coat because the terrace there was uncovered.

He had to queue behind other latecomers at the gate. As he did so, he wondered what it would have been like to watch a game with his dad. He'd never done it. His dad had never really been a big watcher. Playing was more his thing. He'd even had a trial for Albion once. (Or so he said. Just about everyone's dad on earth has had a trial for some club or other.) But Luke's "educated right foot" and "natural football brain" had to have come from somewhere, and they sure enough hadn't come from his mum.

Just after he squeezed through the turnstile, but before he could even see the pitch, the creepiest sound went up. Luke knew it well: the sudden, strangled noise made by about four hundred delirious people at only *one* end of the ground. The away end. Albion were a goal down already. And it didn't get much better.

Nothing went right for the home team. A crocked Ruel Bibbo was substituted after half an hour. Madman Mort couldn't cope with the ball skidding off the turf. The flat back-four was flat on its back for most of the time. And to say that centre half, Chopper Foggon, was having a stinker would be to give innocent smells a bad name. He was horribly at fault for both of Southend's other goals before half-time. But he still came out for the second half. Benny the Boss just didn't have enough strength in depth to replace him with anyone better.

Southend coasted for the rest of the game.

Albion's Carl Davey stabbed the ball home from a corner for a consolation goal, but some of the drenched people around Luke were chanting *Webb Out! Webb Out!* before then, and the goal didn't stop them. The atmosphere inside Ash Acre at the final whistle was horrible. It really did look as if Albion might be headed for the Conference.

"How's your father?" Luke's mum asked him when he got home.

"He's OK." Luke was rubbing at his drowned-rat hair with a towel from the kitchen.

"My goodness, boy! Look at the state of your clothes. I thought he was playing at a pub, not an open-air festival."

"I got wet on my bike," Luke said, but she didn't look convinced.

"Go and get changed at once. No, have a bath first. You look just like one of those idiotic yobs who pay money to go and stand and catch their deaths just so that they can watch overgrown children in silly outfits hoof a bit of animal skin about."

Yep, thought Luke on his way up the stairs, That's my game. And I love it.

8

"Did you see it? Did you see it! God, you must be well gutted!"

"See what?" asked Luke, screwing up his face. It was registration on the first Monday back at school and half a dozen kids were jumping all around him.

"Don't you *read* the papers?" they asked.

"It depends which bits," Luke answered, truthfully.

"The *football* bits."

"You mean Gary Lineker getting a knighthood?" (Luke's mum went crazy when she saw that in the New Year's Honours List. "*For services to FOOTBALL!*" she'd hollered. "I know how *I'd* serve football. Barbecued on a skewer and burnt to a crisp!")

"Nah dummy, not that. Don't you know? Five blokes in that rubbish Castle Albion squad of yours went out on Saturday night and started a big pub fight. Three of 'em got arrested and the other two ended up in hospital. 'The Fisticuff

Five', the papers are calling them. Benny Webb's suspended the lot on no pay and put them all on the transfer list!"

"Which five?" asked Luke, struggling to think of even two Albion players that another club might want to buy.

They sang out the names: not Ruel, not Madman, not Gaffer, not Chrissie Pick or Carl Davey (and not, unfortunately, Chopper Foggon either). It amazed Luke that any of them had the energy to fight after they had looked so dead on their feet against Southend. They must have been saving themselves. But now the club's small squad would be stretched to the limit.

The day dragged slowly by. Most of the teachers seemed fed up to be back, but nowhere near as fed up as the kids. In the afternoon they had a woman student who tried to keep them quiet by saying she was a Villa supporter. Some supporter. She didn't even know they were playing Albion in the Cup next Saturday. Luke was determined to find a way of watching that one, even if it was only on TV.

At the end of school he went to chess club, but after one game he lost interest and trudged out to the bike sheds. "Oh, *there* you are," said two kids from his class. "There's some bloke at the school gates asking for you. He's been there about half an hour."

"What? Who?"

"It's Benny Webb," shouted a girl in a Blackburn bobble hat. "The Soccer Supremo. He must be trying to bribe people to come and watch his sad team."

Luke wheeled his bike round to the entrance. On the way, Cool Frederick fell into step with him. Luke wasn't quite sure why, but Cool Frederick didn't keep the same school hours as anyone else. He seemed to arrive at about eleven in the morning and usually stayed till around five. That was just his schedule, but it didn't do him any harm. His schoolwork was always as sharp as his haircut.

Benny Webb was hopping from foot to foot in the cold – as if he were trying to avoid more little free transfers from the redstarts. He had the signing-on forms in his hand again. Luke smiled and introduced his friend to the manager.

"Respect, Boss," said Cool Frederick.

"Hello, son," said Benny, then he turned at once to Luke. "Look, I won't mess about. We're struggling to put a team out for the Hartlepool game tomorrow night. If we could just get a signature on these papers, I'd take you up there and put you on the subs' bench. If you're good enough, you're old enough. What do you say?"

For a moment Luke couldn't say anything at all. Sub! For a Nationwide League game! He stood gaping for so long that Cool Frederick had to nudge him. "Oh... Well..." Luke gasped. "It's still my mum. You see..."

"Your dad, man. Ask your dad," Cool Frederick said. "He's in town, right?"

"How do you know that?" asked Luke, finding his voice.

"It was in the *Evening Argus*. He's calling himself 'Green' now, right? It was at his gig that it all went off on New Year's Eve."

"The fight? It was at the Four Horseshoes?" Luke was grinning now.

"'Fraid so, son," answered Benny, shaking his head in embarrassment. "So could we have a word with your dad, then? That sounds promising. Seven o'clock tonight? You say where."

Luke gazed from Benny to Cool Frederick. Again he was stuck for words.

"It's too good a chance," Cool F told him. "Take it, man."

When someone as cool as Frederick was sounding this keen, Luke knew he had to think again. "Well," he said slowly. "My dad's actually staying at the Four Horseshoes. We could meet there, I suppose."

"Sorted," said Cool Frederick as he loped away. "And you can tell your mum you're staying over at my place when you go to Hartlepool.'

Benny Webb got into his car and drove off

with a wave. Luke's heart missed a beat at the thought of his mum ever finding out about this. In two hours time he would be sitting in a den of iniquity. With a bloke with a beard. And they would be talking about football. A triple whammy if ever there was one.

9

It turned out to be just a double whammy. Luke, his dad and Benny Webb didn't have their meeting in the Four Horseshoes. The landlord wouldn't let them. He was still mad about the damage caused by the Albion players on New Year's Eve. So when he saw their manager walk in, he showed him the red card right away.

"That was out of order," said Luke's dad in the car park. He was leaning up against his multi-coloured transit van. Even in the dark it made Luke queasy to look at it.

Before Benny's arrival he'd told his dad the whole Albion story, and he seemed pretty chuffed about it. The poor bloke needed something to cheer him up. Luke had read the report about the fight in his dad's paper. A barmaid said the players had started the rumpus because they were bored to tears by the music.

"So where shall we go now?" asked Benny Webb.

"Where do you usually go for talks with star

players that you want to sign?" Luke's dad asked back.

"Well, motorway service stations as a rule. That's easiest when they're comin' from other parts of the country."

"Right then." Luke's dad rubbed his hands together. "There's a Welcome Break twenty-five miles out of town to the east. We'll meet you there."

"Dad, that's ridiculous," Luke protested. If just the look of his dad's van made him feel ill, a forty-minute trip inside it would almost certainly finish him off.

"No, Luke," his dad said, already unlocking the back of the van for Luke to get in. (The passenger seat was stacked with amps and speakers.) "We've got to do this thing the right way."

The journey seemed to take all night. Luke started feeling as sick as a parrot after ten minutes. He got to the service station without throwing up, but then he needed to walk around a bit to recuperate. Meanwhile Benny and his dad bought some tea and Danish pastries and got down to brass tacks. By the time Luke went back to join them, all he had to do was sign his name.

Benny stood and shook Luke by the hand. "Welcome to the club, son," he said. "You won't regret this move. Castle Albion might be Nationwide League minnows at this moment in time. But I have a dream for the future. We're going to build a club to rival the Tottenhams and the Chelseas of this world. We intend to do it by stickin' to all the game's purest principles. And we're gonna begin by reaping three points at Hartlepool United tomorrow night."

"Which could be a problem," said Luke, whose head still felt muzzy. "Will I need time off school tomorrow afternoon to get there for the kick-off? Hartlepool's a long way away, isn't it?"

His dad looked back at him. "Yeah, er... It's on the south coast, right?"

"Well, it is on the coast," said Benny Webb. "But it's right up in the north-east. Just past Middlesbrough. So yes, you'll definitely need the afternoon off."

"No sweat," said Luke's dad. "I'll write the teacher a note. I'll say he's got a dentist's appointment. I mean, this isn't going to happen often, is it?"

Benny looked at him hard. "Put it this way, Mr Green – it might. If your boy's as good as I think he is, it might have to happen quite a lot. And that's why Castle Albion's own Centre of Excellence is starting up a special educational programme for risin' young stars like Luke. That way, they don't have to miss out on *any* of their schooling. Our fully-trained staff will ensure they keep up with all their subjects whilst they're in the care of the club." He turned to Luke. "Now what lessons would you be missin' tomorrow afternoon, son?"

Luke tried to remember his timetable. "History," he said. "Double History actually. And history homework too." A good afternoon to miss out on.

"Leave that with me," said Benny Webb. "But bring your books. Now, one other thing. Since this is all very new, would you like your dad to come along too?"

"Ah, now that would be difficult," his dad cut in. "I'm playing a gig at the Marquis of Granby. Sixties Night. Otherwise I'd love to come."

"Well is there anyone else you'd like to bring along, son? Just for moral support. One of your mates, even? What about that lad I met at the school with you?"

"Cool Frederick?" Luke wondered about that. It might be nice to have *someone* his own age along, even if Frederick acted more grown-up than half the players did. And Luke had already mentioned to his mum that he would be staying with Cool F tomorrow night, to work on a Biology project. "Yes all right, I'll ask him."

Benny shook their hands again and stood up. "This is a historic moment," he said. "In years to come, people will look back on this signing as the beginning of a whole new chapter in the story of football. The start of an era like that of the Busby Babes, or Alf Ramsey's Wingless Wonders."

Then he noticed an embarrassed-looking teenaged cashier who had been hovering near by for a few minutes. There was a pen and a bit of paper in his hand. Benny Webb smiled at him.

"Autograph hunter, eh?" he said. "But it's not my autograph you want, son. It's this boy's here. I'm tellin' you – he's going to be huge. Bigger than Owen."

"I don't want anyone's autograph," the cashier replied in a huff, stepping up to the table. "I made a mistake and only charged you for one of the Danish pastries. You'll have to alter the amount on your cheque. Just put your initials by the changes, OK?"

After that, Luke and his dad watched Benny leave in a swirl of sheepskin. "I think you're in good hands there," said his dad. "And between you and me, I reckon your mum will think so too when she finally gets to hear about it. She's not really as fierce as she makes out, you know."

Luke kept watching Benny go. If his dad had just said, "John Hartson walks on water *and* he's actually from one of the lesser moons of Venus," he would have been more inclined to believe him.

Luke got to Ash Acre as the team coach for Hartlepool was about to leave. The Maths teacher had kept the class behind until someone owned up to stealing his extra pair of winter socks. But in the end he found he'd packed them in his own lunch box. Cool Frederick was already on board – having given school a miss altogether.

"You made it then, son?" Benny said through the gap between Luke and Frederick's headrests as they set off. "Brought your school stuff, have you?"

Luke pointed to his bulging bag. He had to write two sides on Queen Elizabeth I's war with Spain by first thing the next morning. "Good lad," said Benny. "We'll call you for the lesson once we're properly under way – and when that lot back there have quietened down a bit."

The players were making an unbelievable racket. Every couple of minutes they would burst into a deafening chant of:

"We're On Our Way To Hartley...
On Our Way To Hartley..."

In between, Madman Mort did impersonations of the engine sounds made by various fighter planes, and after each one he whined "Are we there yet, Mum?" Meanwhile Chrissie Pick set his ghetto-blaster to top volume, and then it was hard to say what made more noise: his bootleg live Prodigy tape or everyone else screaming at him to turn it off. "And these are just the quieter players," Luke grinned at Cool Frederick, who was finishing off some maths problems. If the so-called "Fisticuff Five" had been on the trip, the coach's roof might have blown off before they reached the motorway.

Half an hour later, though, most of them had dropped off to sleep. Luke kept looking round in his seat to see some sign of the Albion Centre of Excellence's special educational staff. As far as he could see, there were only the players, Benny, and Terry Vaudeville the Physio. Maybe they kept the teachers in the storage section with the kit. Luke wouldn't have been surprised. The kids at school reckoned the deputy head was stuffed in a gym locker at the end of each term.

"Right then," came Benny Webb's voice again, from a bit further back. "Ready for you now, son."

Luke got up and began to drag his bag behind him along the gangway. Madman was sprawled out across two seats near by – everyone else having refused to sit next to him. As Luke passed Benny Webb he smiled but the manager called him back. To Luke's surprise, he patted the empty seat beside him. "Here you go, son," he said. "Park yourself down."

"But what about my lesson?" Luke asked, sitting. There wasn't much room for him to squeeze in because Benny still had his enormous coat on.

"Your lesson, yes. Well, as of this moment, I have to say – with regret – that not every single feature of the educational programme is fully in place. The Centre of Excellence is a relatively recent development at the club, and we are in fact still lookin' to fill one or two key positions within the organization."

Luke looked at him and nodded. "Like the History teacher?"

Benny looked back. "In all honesty, son, like any sort of teacher. We are working on it. I'd been hoping to bring my godson along for you today. He's got a degree in History from Exeter University. But he had a gardening accident last night." His face became as long as Rodney's. "So just this once, I'm afraid, it'll have to be me. Now – what period are we in?"

After two minutes discussion, Luke saw that it

didn't really matter what historical period he was studying – Benny Webb was equally unfamiliar with them all. He might have known who knocked Gillingham out of the FA Cup in 1970 and what year Port Vale came into the League. But even Luke didn't mix up Queen Elizabeth I with Queen Elizabeth II, as the Soccer Supremo kept on doing. And Luke was fairly sure that the Spanish Armada wasn't a burrowing animal with bony plates all over its body.

"Isn't that an armadillo, Boss?" he asked politely.

"Ah, could be, could be. I'm a bit rusty, I must admit. History wasn't really my subject when I went on day release to college. Now if this was joinery..."

"Hey chill out," Frederick called back to them from his seat. He was holding up a battered textbook. "I used this. Tells you everything. Really kicks in."

"That's probably the best way, son," Benny said to Luke. "Back you go."

For the next couple of hours, with a stop for "refuelling", Luke read and wrote like a demon. He'd never lavished so much time on his history before; there were even some moments when he almost enjoyed it. But the best moment of all was when he was able to return Cool F's paperback, put away his exercise book and start to look out for Hartlepool on the horizon.

"Not long now, lads," Benny Webb came and said, leaning on Luke's headrest. To the rear, the chanting started up again. And Madman was giving off a low hum that could have erupted at any time into a Spitfire or a Messerschmidt 109.

"It's not a bad ground, Hartlepool's," Benny went on. "They've done it up a lot. Well, they had to. Now there's a bit of history I *do* know. It was during the First World War. These German zeppelins – you know, big airships? – they dropped bombs on the 'Pool grandstand. First football ground ever to be hit."

"Airships, eh?" said Madman, pricking up his ears from across the gangway. Now Luke didn't have the faintest idea what a World War One zeppelin sounded like. But it must have been pretty close to the wailing, booming hullabaloo that suddenly stormed out of the awesome throat of Madman Mort – until Gaffer Mann, Terry the Physio and Chopper Foggon all came barging up from the back and sat on him.

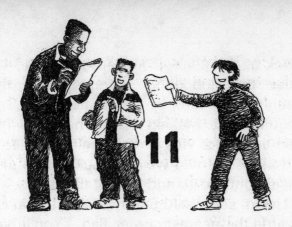

Luke had never been to another club's ground before. It was dark before they got there so he couldn't see much of the outside. There were quite a few people milling about. Some of them booed and hissed as the Albion players stepped down from the coach.

"Good evening, *Hartlepool*!" yelled Chrissie Pick with a grin and a pop-star wave as huge as his stack of hair. You'd never have guessed he had played only three games for the Albion. Then Ruel Bibbo was mobbed by kids wanting autographs. As Luke and Cool Frederick squeezed their way through and followed Benny Webb into the Victoria Ground, a man in a club blazer put out an arm to bar their way.

"Players and officials only, lads," he said. This was getting to be a habit.

"They're OK," Benny Webb called back. But Cool Frederick said he would go and take his seat anyway. He had a few calls to make on his mobile. Everyone else went straight out to take a look at the pitch. It looked brilliant to Luke under the floodlights, even though there weren't many fans in the stadium yet. Some seagulls were making Madman noises overhead and there was a really salty taste to the cold air. It seemed weird to Luke to be at the seaside but not go and look at the sea.

"Listen, son," said Benny Webb, taking Luke towards the nearest corner flag. "You'll be on the bench tonight but I'll only give you a run-out if things get desperate. We ought to be all right. Hartlepool ain't too clever themselves at the moment. Anyway, it's all good experience for you, right?"

"Right, Boss."

"We'll have to get you a club blazer too," Benny added thoughtfully. "That duffel coat and scarf don't look right when you're out inspecting the pitch. Go and get your kit on now."

Luke found the away team's dressing room in uproar. All the players seemed to have lost something vital – shin-pads, bootlaces, tie-ups, chewing gum, the smelly embrocation they rubbed on their legs. But like Luke's Maths teacher they kept on finding them after blaming everyone else in sight.

For a few wild minutes Madman put everyone through the latest goal-celebration routine he had worked out. Then Carl Davey – fully-changed before everyone else – opened up a white Marks and Spencer's bag and took out a pineapple. "Craig!" he yelled, tossing it over to the full-back.

"What's this for?" asked Craig Edwards with a frown.

Carl turned around and pointed at his bottom. "Chuck it at me."

"What?" Everyone looked at him as if he'd lost his marbles.

"Chuck it at me," Carl repeated calmly. "Like you did before training last Thursday. After that, I had my best game of the season against Southend. Scored too. If you do it again, I might score tonight an' all. Go on."

Gleefully Craig coiled back his arm and let fly. Carl's roar must have rung all round the ground. "Thank you kindly," he said when the pain died down.

"And if you don't score in the first forty-five minutes," Gaffer Mann called across, "we'll all take a shot at you during half-time."

"Right lads, listen up," said Benny, clapping his hands. And he launched into a team talk that was so long and complicated that even Clever Trevor Brooking would have had a job understanding it. Each player in turn was given a list of do's and don'ts. Mostly don'ts. In Madman's case, all don'ts.

Lastly Benny turned to Luke, perched on the bench in his kit and trainers between Ruel Bibbo and Dennis Meldrum. "As for you, son, if you do come on, I just want you to play your natural game." He tapped his head and winked. "I know you've got it up here. Now get your boots on, there's a good lad."

Luke swallowed. "But I haven't got any boots."

Another chorus of "*What?*" went around the small room.

"I've never had any," he explained. "My mum's never let me. And I wouldn't be able to stand up on studs now even if I had them."

Benny Webb closed his eyes and rubbed a hand across his forehead. But at that point the referee knocked and came in. "I want a good, clean game tonight," he said. "Or else you'll see so much red and yellow you'll think it's autumn all over again. And as for *you*," he pointed his whistle at Chopper Foggon, "if you make another tackle like you did the last time I had you lot, I won't just send you off, I'll take you to the vet's and have you put down as well."

He disappeared, leaving the door open. "Get out there now, lads," said Benny Webb with his fist clenched. "Keep it simple but keep surprising them! Play with pride for the shirts on your backs! Show the world that the sleeping giant of

Castle Albion is startin' to stir! Oh, and don't give away any cheap corners."

"Yeahhh!" bawled eleven psyched-up but slightly confused players and two substitutes as they headed down the tunnel. Luke, raring to go, just smiled.

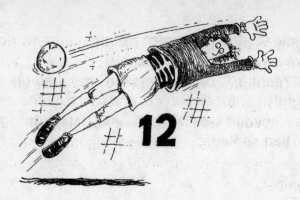

12

Hartlepool went ahead in the twenty-seventh minute. Up till then Albion had looked the better side. But when the home team applied their first bit of pressure, Chopper Foggon sliced a clearance behind to give them a corner.

As the cross came in, Albion's marking was woeful. But that didn't really matter, since the ball wafted over everyone's heads, changed course in a sudden sea-breeze, then swung directly into the top of Madman's net. Luke had never been sure what a hard goal was, but that one had "soft" written all over it.

Benny Webb seemed to shrivel up on the bench next to him.

**"You're Not Singing... You're Not Singing...
You're Not Singing Any More!"**

roared the delighted Hartlepool faithful – although to be fair, Albion's one hundred and twenty-eight travelling supporters would have needed a megaphone to be heard, even if they'd had anything to sing about.

Benny asked Luke and the other subs to sprint up and down the touchline for a while. When the home fans saw Luke they all pointed at him and sang:

"You Need – To Wear – A Nappy!"

Their team was really cooking now, and twice more before the interval they almost scored again.

The second time, their winger broke clean through, only to lose concentration as Madman dashed out. Instead of spreading out his hands, the goalie seemed to yank up his own jersey for a split second. "Surely," gasped Luke with a grin, "he's not wearing. . .?"

"His lucky skeleton chest?" sighed Benny. "Yes. He is. With some of 'em it's pineapples. With others it's painted latex. It was never like this in my day."

At half-time the players weren't as downcast as Luke had expected. Several were still working on the goal-celebration routine. Luke watched as Benny went around to each of them, saying exactly the same things he'd said before the game began. They would all frown and nod seriously, then get back down to their choreography.

"I sometimes wonder if they hear a word I say," Benny told him as they settled down in the dug-out for the second half. "If we don't get one back in half an hour, son, you're on. Ruel's about as mobile as a lamppost up there, but the bloke who's marking him looks scared. We've got to give him proper crosses."

But the crosses didn't come. For long periods the ball went nowhere near the Hartlepool goal. It didn't go near the Albion goal much either. Anyone looking in from Mars might have thought the object of the game was to whack the ball against the advertising boards as often as possible – and that when Luke jogged up and down the touchline, he was providing a moving target. If he had been, though, no one on either side would have had the accuracy to hit him.

Then it happened. Seventeen minutes from the final whistle, Chrissie Pick went on a run down the right. Two Hartlepool defenders converged on him just past the halfway line. The first slid in and cannoned the ball out of play against the *F* in an advert for *Hartlepool's Finest Nite-Spot*. Not to be outdone, the second slid in straight after and clattered Chrissie himself into the *H-a-r-t*.

Benny Webb knew that the YTS lad had kicked his last ball into touch for that evening. "Get your top off, son," he said to Luke as Terry the Physio went to help a dazed and confused Chrissie back to the dressing room. Half a minute later Luke was pattering out on to the hallowed Hartlepool turf in his trainers.

"Son!" Benny shouted at him. And in twisting around, Luke lost his footing on a slick of mud and skidded down on his bottom.

"He Don't – Know – How To Walk Yet!" screamed the home fans. "Don't run about too much," Benny yelled. "Just hit Ruel's head as soon as you get it."

With nine minutes left on the clock, Luke did the business. A home defender thumped away a hopeless Carl Davey cross, but Luke trapped the ball before it hit the hoardings. Glancing up, all he could see at the far post was Ruel Bibbo. His head seemed to be the size of a zeppelin – Luke simply couldn't miss it. Over went the cross, up went the airship. Hartlepool one, Castle Albion one.

Luke was still outside the penalty area as the long-awaited celebration unfolded in front of the delirious one hundred and twenty-eight. He didn't rush to join in. This was nothing like the rehearsal in the dressing room. The players were meant to form a train, with each one's head stuck up the back of the shirt of the man in front. Pretty soon the whole thing got derailed. In the resulting pile-up Gaffer Mann nearly broke his neck. And Ruel was limping even more heavily when he got to his feet.

Eight minutes to go. Seven. Six. A draw wasn't a lot of use to Albion. They needed all three points – and as the one hundred and twenty-eight kept on squealing, the 'Pool were now there for the taking. Luke got the ball a couple more times – standing still and spraying inch-perfect passes to Ruel and Carl. There was no way he was going to try to run on that treacherous surface. Three minutes left, two.

Ruel tried a speculative shot from thirty-five yards. The keeper misjudged it but managed to scramble it around the post for a corner.

"Let the kid take it!"
piped the one hundred and twenty-eight. Luke was already trotting across to the flag. Twice he nearly slipped on the way there. He didn't take a run-up to the kick – just swung back his leg and aimed at where that great big zeppelin was going to rise up.

But this time Ruel's groin-strain meant he didn't spring quite so high as before. The defender went up with him. The ball got lodged between their heads. Then it spilled down to the waiting Carl "Pineapple" Davey who volleyed it home.

Forgetting all about the train routine, a frenzied Carl ran the length of the pitch grinning fit to burst and pointing at his bottom. The ref finally caught up with him and booked him for making what seemed to be obscene gestures. The Albion didn't care. Half a minute later the final whistle went. Two-one, two-one, two-one, two-one! They had stormed Fortress Hartlepool and come away with three priceless points!

13

The journey home was massively long, incredibly noisy and fantastically good fun.

"Normally we'd stay over till the morning," Benny explained to Luke and Cool Frederick as they headed south again. "But the club's so strapped for cash just now, we can't even afford to spend the night in a YMCA."

Luke didn't mind. He would never have slept anyway. All he kept seeing were those two crosses of his zooming into the box. "You really made the difference, son," Terry the Physio came up and told him on the coach. And since the final whistle, everyone else – even Chopper Foggon – had clapped him on the back and congratulated him on his outstanding debut.

They stopped seven times on the way home. "If Nature calls any more, it'll start to lose its voice," Benny Webb sighed. At one service station they all had a full English breakfast, which Luke wolfed back like a player twice his size.

"Here we are, look!" Craig Edwards yelled, coming out of John Menzies with a first edition of the *Daily Mail*. He held up the back page.

"*England Squad Put On Loaves and Fishes Diet*," read a puzzled Gaffer Mann.

"No, not that! Here!" Craig pointed at a tiny box in the corner – a ten-line report on the Hartlepool-Albion match. The headline just said: *STUDLESS SENSATION*. The players all whistled and hooted at Luke who smiled down proudly at his greasy plate. "*An inspired substitution by manager Benny Webb changed the course of the match*," read Craig. "*The youngest-ever player in British football broke the deadlock with a stream of pinpoint passes. Who knows how far he'll go when they let him play in a pair of boots?*"

His team-mates mobbed him then. And once they were back on the road – in between chants of *Bring On The Villa!* – Madman led them in a top-volume chorus which went: "Give us an L! Give us a U! Give us a K! Give us an E! Then what have you got?"

"The Studless Sensation!"

"I think they like you, son," smiled Benny Webb as they stopped for the last call of Nature. They were standing in a big service station car park and some of the players were tapping a ball around. As Cool Frederick went over to join in, a bit of snow was starting to swirl in the grey dawn air. "I hope the weather holds for Sunday," Benny went on. "We want a crack at the Villa while our tails are still up. You're gonna be all right for Sunday, son, aren't you?"

"Yes, Boss," said Luke. It wasn't going to be easy though. His nan and grandpa were coming for the weekend. And Luke wasn't sure how he was going to give everyone the slip between two o'clock and five. On top of that, the *Daily Mail* was the paper his mum read, and his stomach flipped over when he thought of her catching a glimpse of his name as she rabidly screwed up the sports pages later that morning.

"Stone *me*!" said Benny suddenly. "That mate of yours knows what to do with a ball, don't he? What do they feed you at that school?"

Luke glanced across the car park and grinned when he saw Cool F playing keepy-uppy with his knees, thighs, shoulders, head and heels. Then when the passing game started again, the quality of his distribution made the other players in the ring look distinctly Dr Martens League.

"Next Monday, son," Benny said to Frederick after calling them all back to the coach, "would you be interested in coming for a trial at Ash Acre?"

"Happenin'," said Frederick with a dip of his head as he went back to his seat.

"Does that mean yes?" Benny Webb asked Luke, who laughed and nodded.

The coach finally dropped Luke and Frederick two roads away from their school. There were fifteen minutes to go till registration so there was no need to hurry. One or two kids pretended to fall off their bikes next to Luke at the shock of Albion actually winning a game. But no one then or later in the day seemed to have spotted that he'd been playing. Third Division matches didn't get a write-up in most papers – especially when there were in-depth articles to be written about Graeme Le Saux's latest haircut and Man U's unveiling of their fifth away strip of the season. That was a big relief. Luke could only pray that his escapade had escaped his mum's notice too.

By four o'clock his late night was catching up with him. He dozed most of the way through PSE, and the kid next to him said that he was snoring in Science. No change there, then. He wanted to go straight to bed as soon as he got home.

His heart skipped a beat when he saw a Volvo parked outside his house. Then he saw it was only his Auntie Evelyn's. Sometimes she gave his mum a lift back from town after a particularly gruelling tour of the shops. But when Luke got indoors, he knew there was something wrong. *Badly* wrong.

An odd sound was coming from the kitchen. The kind of noise a light bulb makes just before it pops. Crackly, buzzy, fizzy, hummy.

This wasn't a light bulb on its last legs, though. This was Luke's mum. He could hear his Auntie Evelyn trying to calm her down: "Leave it, love... Don't work yourself up... It must all be a terrible mistake..." None of it did any good.

"*Luke!*" his mum screeched in a strangled voice. "Get in here!"

Luke didn't look at his mum or aunt as he slid around the door. His eyes were glued to the table where they were sitting. In the middle of it sat an opened box of the most beautiful Adidas Predator boots. He could smell the sweet leather even from the doorway. Next to them was a small calling card. Scribbled on it in appalling handwriting was the following message:

Luke, You don't know me but now that you're a star you're going to need an agent. Please accept these boots as a kick-off. There's plenty more where they came from, I can tell you. We can do LOADS of beautiful business together. Lolly, son, loads of lovely lolly. I'll call again later today. Yours, Neil Veal.

Ceasing to breathe as his mum hummed louder, Luke turned over the card.

On that side, this had been printed:

Agent Veal

The Cash Is Out There

(All I ask is Ten Per Cent*)

*Rising to 25% for Supermarket Openings and Computer-Game Endorsements

---

"I think, Luke," said his aunt nervously, "that your mother deserves an explanation."

14

Luke told his mum the lot. Well, everything except the bit about his dad signing the forms. He didn't see why the poor guy should have to die too. Spilling the beans seemed the only way. But the more he said, the more he felt like the Spanish Armada, sinking deeper and deeper in the water. Even so, the Spanish Armada just had to sink quietly. It didn't have to put up with the added horror of watching somebody's mum about to blow apart.

"...And so we got back from Hartlepool just before school this morning," Luke said, coming to the end of the story so far, his eyes flitting between the two open-mouthed women. "Oh – but I did get my history homework in."

Not surprisingly, this last fact did not make his mum smile with joy and tell him it made up for everything else. Instead, still buzzing, she began to do something odd with her fist on the kitchen table – opening and closing her fingers as if she were practising to wring his neck.

Auntie Evelyn understood. She sprang up, sloshed a huge amount of his mum's favourite cooking sherry into a mug marked *Penzance* and wedged it into her hand.

"Hartlepool..." murmured Luke's mum before glugging back a mouthful. "Hartlepool?" Another mum-sized glug. "*Hartlepool!*"

"Easy now, easy," soothed Auntie Evelyn, looking panicky. She stepped back smartly to the sink. Then she put her hand on the cold tap (was she getting into position to hose her sister down the minute she burst into flames?).

"You *played* ... in a *professional* ... *football* match?" his mum muttered into her mug, as if she was accusing the terrified inch of sherry still trembling there.

"Well, only for the last few minutes," Auntie Evelyn cut in, the tension starting to get to her. "Isn't that what you said, Luke? That you were only a sub...?"

"You *PLAYED* ... in a *PROFESSIONAL* ... *FOOTBALL* match?"

Slowly Luke nodded his head. Auntie Evelyn shrank smaller against the sink. If she could have crawled up *inside* the cold tap, she looked as if she might have given it a try. One last big glug and all the sherry was gone. With her lips clamped tight, his mum buzzed louder than ever as she raised herself to her feet. And somehow the buzzing continued when she then hissed at Luke: "You are telling me that you have been going behind my back? For *months*? That you have been lying to me all along in order to go to that infernal *place*? And that now – *now* – you are actually mixing with the scum that *plays* the filthy game?"

Luke wouldn't have described it quite that way, but that was definitely the general picture. "Yes, Mum. I'm sorry, Mum."

Then it happened: "*AAAARRRRGGGGHHHH!*"

Luke shut his eyes tight as soon as the single, awesome roar erupted from her throat. It climbed to a floodlight-fusing peak then trailed away in a ragged, drawn-out snarl – just like the noise fans make to put off a keeper as he runs up to take a goal kick. Only this was louder than anything he'd ever heard at Ash Acre. And something else was different too. As it faded, a metallic rattling sound started up, followed by a dull thump – then a long, whining creak.

Luke opened his eyes expecting to find a medieval siege engine sprouting out of his mum's gaping mouth. But it had only been the front door sticking as Rodney let himself in from work. Holding his lunch box, he appeared in the kitchen doorway with a nervy smile. "Having one of your headaches, are you dear?" he asked Luke's mum as the echo of her scream finally died.

She drooped over the table, panting, gasping,

hardly hearing – winding herself up for another absolute belter.

"Easy, easy..." pleaded Auntie Evelyn, slinking away from the sink and trying to press herself back among the parsnips and carrots on the lower vegetable shelf. "Look, Rodney's brought a visitor."

"Ah, yes," Rodney said. "I found him out on the doorstep." He stood aside to reveal a tall spotty guy in his late teens, wearing a suit so sharp you could have used it to chop firewood. "He says he has an appointment with *you*, Luke."

"Yes indeedy," grinned the stranger, flashing at least three golden teeth. With one long stride he entered the room, offering his hand. Luke backed away. Stalking closer, the stranger grinned even wider. "Veal's the name. Agent Neil Veal. I believe that you and I have a small fortune to make!"

Luke never got to shake his hand. From the corner of his eye he saw his mum swoop down on the box of Adidas Predators, snatch one up and hurl it with stunning force at the visitor's head. Agent Veal staggered, making a funny little noise like a hungry budgie. Seeing stars, he turned to where the missile had come from and – lo and behold – Predator number two came crashing into his other temple.

Even at the time, Luke had to marvel at his

mum's accuracy. This was the kind of boot-to-head strike ratio that hard men like Chopper Foggon would die for.

"*Leave my house!*" growled Luke's mum so ferociously that both Auntie Evelyn and Rodney automatically edged backwards. "We have nothing to say to you now, and nothing to say to you *ever*! *GET OUT!*"

Agent Veal – crouching, barely conscious – raised an arm to shield his head, just in case she started flinging her own shoes. He flashed a lopsided grin up at Luke and somehow managed to wink before backing out. "Not a good time, obviously," he whispered. "You've got my card. Let's do lunch."

"Shut the door after him, Rodney!" Luke's mum ordered. Then she turned to Luke, waving at the boots, "And you. Pick up those ... *things.*" By the time he had done so, she was standing over the swing-bin, holding back its lid. "In there." The leather felt gorgeous under Luke's fingers. Sluggishly he crossed the floor and dropped the boots into the rubbish. They fell on a screwed-up, teabag-stained *Daily Mail* back page. *STUDLESS SENSATION* cried the headline in the little match-report box. His mum let the lid swing shut. "And listen to me now," she said, "and listen to me hard. You will never, never, never, *never*, *NEVER* play football again! Is that understood?"

But before Luke could say a word in reply, she threw back her head and out it came: "*AAAAAAARRRRRRGGGGGGGGHHHHHHH!*"
Then Rodney reappeared in the doorway, still clutching his lunch box. "Let me get you an Anadin, dear," he said, quivering.

15

"So it's a permanent suspension, then?" asked Cool Frederick as the Maths teacher blathered on about logarithms over by the blackboard.

"Life ban," shrugged Luke. "And no chance of an appeal."

"Heavy-duty bummer. What about the Boss – does he know? He's got you down to play from the off against the Villa, right?"

"Not any more, he hasn't. My mum sent him a sort of death threat. Auntie Evelyn delivered it to the ground last night. She told him if he ever said another word to me she'd prosecute him for corrupting a minor. And she would too."

"Naughty. But hey, there's gotta be some way round this."

"I don't think so. Not now. I really don't think so..."

"You boys!" the maths teacher yelled. "You two by the radiator. Yes, *you*!" He had only been teaching them for a term – not long enough to learn Luke and Frederick's names. "Shut up, will you! I'm *talking*. Show some respect."

Luke and Frederick exchanged weary glances as they turned to face the front. They did their best but it wasn't easy to respect a man who kept socks in his sandwich box.

"There's *gotta* be a way," Frederick softly repeated.

They met up again on their way out of school that afternoon. "Look at this," said Luke, showing Frederick the essay on Queen Elizabeth I he had just been given back. "Straight A. She said it was the best bit of work I'd ever done."

"Respect to the Castle Albion Centre of Excellence."

Luke grinned, but when they got to the gates he slowed down and his shoulders sagged.

"Hey, don't let it get to you, man," said Frederick. "I told you, I know there's got to be some way around this. Your mum's only one woman."

"Yeah, but you haven't heard the kind of noise she can make."

Frederick smiled and flipped up his hood as it started to rain. "We've got to be able to sort this. Grab your bike and let's go get a Coke and talk."

Luke shrugged and shook his head. "No bike

today. Nor any other day. And I'm not allowed to go anywhere except school and home. That's the new deal."

"So we'll talk as we walk."

"No way. Mum doesn't trust me any more. From now on she's going to be ferrying me to and fro – her or Rodney. I've got to wait for him here now. She even said he's got to hang around when I go for dinner with my dad tonight. It's not much fun for Rodney either. He just wants to watch birds."

Frederick raised his eyebrows and blew out his cheeks. The rain came on harder as cars sloshed by to pick up the dozens of kids who were waiting. A Vauxhall Cavalier slowed down right in front of Luke. There was a bright flash of light then the driver sped away. A minute later it happened again with a souped-up Astra.

"Whoa," said Frederick, sucking in his breath. "Paparazzi."

Luke turned away to face the school gates. That was no better. A line of girls from his art class were walking out with linked arms.

"*Ooh*, **Mr Studless!** *Ooh* **Mr Studless!**" they all chanted at him as they passed. It was the ninth time Luke had been sung at that day – including twice by the dinner ladies.

"Face it," grinned Frederick. "You're big news. You're already all over the local papers after what you did at Hartlepool. Soon everyone's gonna want a piece of you. Maybe you *should* check out that agent guy. Look, he's over there."

"Over where?"

"There. That's your man, right?" Luke turned and Frederick pointed to a silver-grey BMW convertible purring up next to the hockey pitch across the road. *Agent Veal – Deals on Wheels* was painted in red letters on the door. And although it was sleeting with rain he had his window down and was looking around for flying Predators before getting out and adjusting his Raybans.

He caught Luke's eye, flashed him a metallic smile and strutted out into the road. Just at that moment Rodney careered around the corner in his 1978 Ford Escort.

He didn't actually run Agent Veal over but it would have been a lot quieter if he had. The brakes screamed, the engine gave out with a magnified burp, and the passenger door clunked open as the car slalomed through a huge puddle. The agent was sprayed from head to moccasined toe with oxtail-coloured water, then whacked all down one side by the door.

He reeled on over to Luke's side of the road, somehow keeping his feet and also – miraculously – the smile on his face. Twisting around, he gave a thumbs-up to the anxious Rodney who was struggling to get his seat-belt off. "No damage.

Just a graze." Then he turned as if to walk past Luke. "I know you've got to go now," he hissed, swaying a little, "but let's do lunch, yeah?"

Luke looked quickly at Rodney, still fighting with his seat-belt. "I can't," he murmured back. "I eat here with all the others, in the hall."

"No stress." The agent was definitely staggering now. "Let's do school lunch."

"Luke!" Rodney called out through the opened passenger-door. "Come on."

"Safe journey," slurred the agent as he turned into the school drive – and immediately collapsed sideways into the dustbin area.

"Go now," urged Cool Frederick. "I'll see if he needs a stretcher. But we need to get our act together. Where are you meeting your dad tonight? And when?"

"At that Harvester opposite the pub where he's staying. Eight o'clock. Why?"

"You'll see. Just tell Birdman Rodney you'd like a few minutes with your dad *alone*. Father-son stuff. Private, you know?" He nodded. "Till later."

16

It was still blitzing down with rain four hours later as Rodney's Escort limped across town to the Harvester. Teatime back at the house hadn't been very jolly. Luke's mum wasn't going *"Aaaarrrrgggghhhh!"* any more but she gave the impression that she could do it in a flash if – say – she saw someone out in the street with a moustache like Desmond Lynam's or thought she could smell the next-door neighbours cooking ghastly-burgers.

Rodney was almost entirely silent after picking up Luke from school. This was weird but at least he hadn't told Luke's mum about Agent Veal showing up again.

"Rodney," Luke began as they creaked to a halt in the Harvester car park. "Would it be OK if I went in to see Dad on my own?" He'd crossed his fingers in both pockets of his duffel coat. "It's sort of ... personal."

Rodney stared through the windscreen as if he hadn't heard. Luke peered harder through the glass himself. Maybe there was a bunch of rare ravens perched up there on the pub sign. "I need to ... sort something out with him," he added. "It won't take long, I promise. Ten minutes, tops." It doesn't sound convincing, Luke thought. He'll never agree to it. He knows this is dodgy.

"Yes all right, Luke," Rodney suddenly said, rubbing his hand across his forehead and bumping it into his glasses. "But first I want you to tell *me* something personal. Just between the two of us. Would you do that?" He was still gazing through the windscreen at the rain, completely in a world of his own. He sounded as if he might be about to cry.

"Yes, sure," said Luke, crossing his fingers tighter.

Rodney swung around in his seat and wrinkled his brow at his stepson. "It's just this, Luke." He scratched his head. "I mean, I don't quite know how to put it." He tried to grin. "But what was it *like*? Running on to the pitch at Hartlepool, playing in front of all those fans? Being out there? Up there? *In* there? What did it *feel* like?"

Luke swallowed hard. Rodney had fixed him with a gaze full of wonder and longing. He had never seen the guy so fired-up without something beaked and feathered flapping about in front of him. "It was brilliant," was all he could truthfully say. "From beginning to end. Absolutely brilliant."

"And how – how can I phrase this? What was the *best* bit – would you say?"

Luke thought. "Probably just being part of the team. Or the coach trip back."

An impish smile stole across Rodney's face, making him look twenty years younger. If he *had* been twenty years younger, he would probably have followed it up with a clenched fist and a *Yessssss!* But he was forty-two, and he was married to a woman who went *Aaaarrrrgggghhhh!* and he was supposed to be a kind of probation officer to the young offender sitting next to him. So he simply shook his head, switched off his smile and turned his face back to the rain. "I just wanted to know," he said. "Now go and see your dad."

The born-again hippie called Green was waiting at a table under a display of old farm tools. Harvesters don't have a dress code but that night they probably wished they did. He was kitted out in an orange polka-dot baggy-sleeved blouse with matching headband and purple crushed-velvet loon pants. "All clear?" he asked before Luke could get his eyes back into focus and draw up a chair.

"Yes, I think so. Rodney's waiting outside in the car for a bit."

"Fab!" Half-standing, he beckoned across to the corner. Moments later they were joined by Cool Frederick and, lurking behind the turned-up collar of his sheepskin coat, Bossman Benny Webb. Luke looked left and right for a glimpse of Agent Veal but there was no sign – yet. They all sat and Frederick passed Luke a Coke. "I told the Boss you'd be here at eight," he explained.

"Cheers, Frederick," said Luke. "And cheers, Boss."

"No trouble, son. Oh, and these are for you." He reached into his coat pocket and handed a ticket each to Cool Frederick and Luke's dad. "Complimentaries for the Villa game on Sunday. Just above the dug-out. I'd *like* to think you'll be feastin' your eyes on the newest and brightest star in Albion's firmament." He gestured at Luke. "But a certain lady has a problem with that, right?"

"Tell me about it," sighed Luke, sipping his Coke. "She says I'll only ever play again over her dead body. But I'm beginning to wonder… There might be a chance of getting Rodney to help. He really seems quite keen on football."

"The Birdman!" guffawed Luke's dad, who had a bit of attitude towards Rodney. "What's his team then? The Magpies? The Seagulls? The Canaries?"

"I'm serious. He seemed really impressed by me playing at Hartlepool."

"We all were," said his dad, patting Luke's hand fondly. "*Ab*fab!"

"I reckon I could work on him a bit," Luke continued, with half his mind staying on birds for a moment. "I'd somehow have to show him what it's *really* like at the Albion. But I can't be too obvious about it."

"The element of surprise, eh?" nodded Benny Webb. "But we're up against the clock on this one. It's Friday tomorrow. The game's on Sunday."

"Right! This is what we do!" said Luke. Suddenly he slapped down his Coke, smiling as Cool Frederick's mobile began to ring and he turned away to take the call. "Is there a training session at the ground on Saturday?"

"Just a light one in the morning, yes," Benny told him. "A forty-five minute practice match then a few set pieces. Ten till twelve."

"Can you leave a side gate unlocked? By the kids' turnstile at the Town End?"

"Sure. Why? Do you think you could get there, then?"

Luke grinned at his dad, his mate, his Boss. "I'll certainly give it my best shot."

17

Friday wasn't the easiest day of Luke's school career. Almost everyone now knew about him playing for the Albion, thanks to a *Luke Green Factfile* in the *Argus*'s build-up to the Villa match – *"the town's biggest sporting event since Princess Anne broke the all-comers' speed record on the ring road."*

The *Factfile* had two good action pics but it was pretty thin on actual facts. All of them came from Luke's write-up as mascot in the Carlisle United matchday programme. It did say, though, that his agent was Neil Veal, who had *"painstakingly nurtured Luke from infancy through to his début, ensuring that Benny Webb played him only when he was completely ready,"* but that *"he was now considering offers for any quality product endorsements, not necessarily connected with sport."* Luke thanked God his mum never bought a local paper.

As one lesson ran into the next, he went on

taking stick. Most of it was fairly good-humoured – except from several teachers who thought he was already earning more money than them. And when the head came towards him in the main downstairs corridor, Luke steeled himself. She was bound to have a go at him for bunking off afternoon school to get to Hartlepool. But she just smiled. "I'll hear if your schoolwork suffers," she said as she passed. And that was it.

Cool Frederick wasn't in school that day so Luke had to hang around at the gates afterwards on his own. Well, not quite on his own. There were also fifty kids in a pyramid by the dustbins, all pointing at him and singing at regular intervals:

"ONE Lukey Green.
There's Only ONE Lukey Green..."

Rodney finally showed up and they drove home in the same strange silence as on the day before – the best possible conditions for Luke to start laying the bait for his stepdad. "I was out on my bike the other day," he said, "and I saw a high-up nest – only I'd never seen anything quite like *these* birds before..."

Rodney's hands tightened on the wheel and he sat further forward in his seat. It was painfully easy to hook him. "Really?" he said. "Describe them to me."

"Well: about the size of sparrows but shaped

more like robins. Mainly greyish, with these long, square tails that were flickering all the time and were sort of – I don't know – rusty-coloured."

Rodney's knuckles had gone white on the steering wheel. He tried to drop two gears to turn the corner into their street but missed and made a horrible scrunching sound. "Their call," he said hoarsely, leaning closer to Luke, "was it like this: *Tak... Tak...* and *Tseep... Tseep...?"*

"Pretty much, I'd say." Though it was hard to be sure above the racket the Escort was making, still grinding along in the wrong gear.

"And their song – did it go..." Rodney then made the most bizarre warbling noise, inter-spersed with a grating rattle that sounded like *churr*. "Was that it?"

"I reckon so."

Rodney slammed on the brakes outside their house, stalling the engine just an inch short of a purple Mondeo that was reversing into the space in front. He bowed his forehead close to the centre of the steering wheel. "*Phoenicurus ochruros,"* he said in a hushed, almost religious voice. "Black redstarts! Winter migrants. I haven't seen a black redstart since October 1967."

"I could show you in the morning," Luke suggested, "if you liked."

"The morning? In the *morning*?" His words

were barely audible; the whole top half of his body was shaking. "Why not right this minute?"

Luke pointed at the two smiling, waving people getting out of the Mondeo up ahead. "Because my nan and grandpa have just arrived for the weekend."

"Right. *Right*." Rodney sat up straighter and pulled himself together. "Tomorrow, though – yes? With the binoculars?"

"How about ten o'clock? We could spot for a couple of hours before lunch."

Rodney took a deep breath. "Ten o'clock would be absolutely perfect."

There was a rapping at the passenger window. Luke turned to see his grandpa banging away at the glass and holding up the *Argus Factfile* – showing a photo of Luke flighting in that corner for the winner at Hartlepool.

"What's all this, then?" the old man demanded in his broad Yorkshire accent as Luke opened the door and got out. "Turning out for *Castle Albion*? What on earth was wrong with good old Doncaster Rovers? Too good for *them*, were you?"

Before Luke could answer, his grandpa hugged him so hard with one arm that he thought he could feel his ribs bend. "Why, it's terrific, Luke lad! I couldn't believe my eyes when I read this. Pleased as punch we were, me and your nan – proud too. But how did you ever get your mother to let you play?"

"Ah now," said Rodney, slamming his own door shut and coming around to shake Luke's nan and grandpa by the hand. "That *is* a bit of a grey area. I really think that, all things considered, it would be best not to say any more on this visit about ... football. And if I were you," he pointed at the newspaper with a very, very worried expression, "I'd leave that in the car."

Grandpa frowned, but then the front door of the house opened and Luke's ashen-faced mum waved from the doorstep. "Hello there," she called. "You got here, then?" She sounded even less lively than one of Trevor Francis's match commentaries.

"Hello, love!" cried Grandpa. And he was just about to wave back with the *Argus* in his hand when Luke snatched it and tossed it into the Escort. He had to. He knew that if his mum caught a glimpse of it, it would turn at once into the *Aaaarrrrgggghhhh-us*. And Luke needed to keep things nice and quiet until he took his stepdad bird-spotting the next morning.

18

Luke slept late on Saturday morning. But at nine forty-five there was a tap at his door and Rodney came in with a mug of tea and some beans on toast.

"I don't know why you're mollycoddling him," Luke's mum shouted from the stairs. But Luke knew. Rodney already had his binoculars around his neck. His tatty bird-spotter's logbook was poking out of his puffer-jacket pocket. And his face was so tense, he could have been lining up at number five in a penalty shoot-out.

"Quarter of an hour, Luke," he said, "then you'll take me to the nest, right?"

"Right." Luke gobbled down his breakfast, closed the door and pulled on his mascot kit. Then he put his usual sweatshirt and tracksuit bottoms over it. He was on his way to the stairs when he heard a "Pssst!" noise from along the landing. "Oh hi, Grandpa," he said, but the old guy wanted him in his room.

"I must have a quick word, lad," he said under

his breath once Luke was inside. "It's about this football business. Your mum told us a bit about it last night – before the steam started coming out of her ears. By heck lad, it's a fine mess. You've got to play in that Villa game, but how? Your mum's organized a trip for us all to the garden centre on Sunday afternoon. How are we going to get you up to Ash Acre and on that pitch?"

Luke smiled, pulling up his top a couple of inches to show the blue-and-white hoops underneath. "I've got a plan, Grandpa. I need to get Rodney on my side, and I think I know how to do it. But if *you* could join in too, when I get back home with him at lunchtime, that would be great."

"Join in what, lad?"

"I think you'll know what to do," said Luke, glancing away as Rodney called to him from the foot of the stairs. "Look, I've got to go. Birds to see."

Grandpa pulled back the door for him. "Well, good luck to you," he whispered. "But maybe if I hadn't taken your mum to watch Doncaster so often when she was a lass, she might never have started hating the game like this. Mind you, Donny Rovers *were* bad. Week in, week out: the absolute pits. But it was loveable rubbish, you know? And now they've gone down to the Conference." He punched Luke playfully hard on the shoulder. "Maybe if you'd started playing for *them* a few years back, they'd still be in the League."

"Luke!" Rodney yelled.

"See you later," Luke grinned through the pain of his grandpa's punch, then he skipped down the stairs rubbing at the sore patch. Now there was a guy who could have shown the Fisticuff Five a thing or two.

Rodney couldn't get the Escort going. The engine was all right – he was just too excited to juggle with the accelerator pedal to keep it alive.

"It's OK," said Luke, "the nest's only up the road. We can walk there in no time."

It was an ice-bright Saturday morning – the start of the season's best weekend. Luke could almost smell it in the air: the FA Cup Third Round! The round when all the big clubs joined in. Man U, Liverpool, Arsenal, Chelsea – and Torquay, Dagenham, York and Northwich Victoria were all there waiting for them.

As Luke strode up the hill – with Rodney twittering on about the five best black redstart spots of his life – fans of all ages were criss-crossing the country on their way to the games. Coachloads from Exeter with dreams of stitching up Middlesbrough. Everton's army wondering just how good Dulwich Hamlet's new strike-force was. No one was taking anything for granted. On this weekend of all weekends anything could happen. *And so often it did!*

Yeovil could beat Arsenal. Spurs could be tanked by Southport. Alan Shearer might fail to find the net against Brighton. Even Aston Villa could come a cropper at Castle Albion in the only game put back to Sunday to be televised live. It was David v Goliath. Jack v the Giant. Luke could hardly stop whooping out loud for thinking about it. *Anything could happen*. And if he did his own stuff right today, then he could be a part of it!

Rodney was describing his fourth-best spot by the time they walked under the nearest floodlight pylon. He hadn't even noticed that they were at Ash Acre. Nor did he pause for a moment as Luke turned off the road and led him up towards the gate he had mentioned to Benny Webb. The only thing that could have lifted Rodney out of his own private dreamworld was a tank-sized golden eagle hovering over the stadium in search of a mid-morning snack.

Benny had done his bit. The blue gate was ajar. Luke went straight through and Rodney followed. It was eerie inside that corner of the ground: utterly empty and silent except for the odd shout wafting over from the pitch. Luke didn't even glance at the grass. He had to hurry Rodney straight along the cinder-track to where the black redstarts were nesting.

"Ohhhhh..." gasped Rodney all of a sudden. Luke stopped dead, fearing the worst. "*Oh-Ohhhhhhh...*" sounded again behind him. The golden eagle had swooped: Rodney had wised up at last to where they were and now he was winding up for a full-blown variation on Luke's mum's *Aaaarrrrgggghhhh*.

"Oh-oh-*ohhhhhhhh...*" gusted past Luke's ear a third time. The game was up. Cringing, he turned to face his speechless stepdad. But before he started to explain, Rodney floated past him, gazing upwards with a face so serene that he could have been watching a small miracle. And, in a way, he was.

He had spotted the black redstarts. As he came level with the players' tunnel, without taking his gaze off the birds, he raised his binoculars to his eyes like a salute. And at once they saluted him back – with a welcoming dollop of mess.

Luke dipped his head in relief. It had worked. The first phase of his plan had gone like a dream. Now for phase two, he told himself, pulling off his sweatshirt.

"Over here, son!" called Benny Webb at the far end of the halfway line.

Luke stood up from taking off his tracksuit bottoms, quickly ran his thumbs under the elastic waistband of his Albion shorts, then trotted across the pitch. As he passed, the players stopped their practice match and watched in delight. "Give us an L!" roared Carl Davey from the Town End penalty area.

"*L!*" the others all yelled.

"Give us an E!"

"*E?*" they bellowed, looking baffled.

"Give us a W!"

"*W?*" Even more baffled.

"And give us a C!"

"*C?*" they stormed. "*What the hell are you on about?*"

"Oh, I dunno how to spell his name!" belted out Carl. "But what have we got?"

"*THE STUDLESS SENSATION!*"

"Am I glad to see you," moaned Benny

Webb. "This lot can shout all right but they've been playing for half an hour and still no one's scored. Sort 'em out for me, will you? Play for Team A. You've got the right shirt on."

Luke took a quick look at Rodney, who seemed to have just realized that his stepson had vanished. Perfect – he would notice him soon enough now.

Play restarted with a dropped ball and it broke back to Gaffer Mann. Waving everyone upfield, the skipper wound back his leg for one of his long, raking through-balls. The opposition hadn't yet worked out who was meant to be marking the newcomer. Luke broke into a sprint, seeing a clear channel ahead.

Gaffer saw it too. He aimed his clearance into the open space. But Third Division centre-halves aren't the most accurate passers in the world. The ball went too high, then began to fall short. Still at full speed, Luke cocked his head and in a split second he looked from the goal in front of him to the ball that was drop-ping down just behind him. It was worth a try – he'd practised this move a few times with Cool Frederick in the park. Spinning himself sideways into the air, he scissored back his left leg then hooked the ball up over his own head – and straight into the net between the keeper and his near post.

Luke didn't remember hitting the ground. It

seemed as if all his team-mates rushed up and caught him – then tossed him even higher in celebration. As he cantered back to his own half afterwards, he glanced over at Rodney. He had his binoculars to his eyes again. But now, just as Luke had hoped, he was training them on the pitch. On him. And even the black redstarts would have understood why.

For the next ten minutes Luke gave a flawless display of all the midfield arts. Tucking in, tackling back, knocking on, laying off. He drove across a low free kick for Ruel Bibbo to tap in a second goal. And just before Benny Webb blew for full time, he nutmegged two defenders on a mazy dribble that took him into the box, only for the keeper to lunge out and knock him for six. Or at least that's what *seemed* to happen. But as Luke somersaulted forwards, he picked up the ball between his ankles then continued to turn head over heels until both boy and ball hit the back of the net.

He clambered to his feet to take another standing ovation – only to find Rodney urgently beckoning him from the touchline. It was hard to be sure from a distance, but he didn't look happy. Luke began the long walk, dreading that phase two of his plan had backfired. "Got to go already, son?" the Boss asked, jogging up behind him. "So how about Sunday? Will you be able to make it?"

"I think I'm just about to find out," Luke said out of the corner of his mouth.

Rodney had put away his binoculars and was standing with folded arms. The look on his face was peculiar – stern and anxious, grown-up and childish all at the same time – and the white splash on his forehead made it look even odder. He began to nod. "I thought I'd seen it all," he said in a low voice that sounded almost menacing. "But I never imagined I would witness anything like *this*."

"*This?*" Benny Webb asked doubtfully from two steps behind Luke.

Rodney flung out his arms. "*THIS!*" He waved at the goal. "*THAT!*" Then with both hands he pointed at Luke. "*YOU!*"

"*Me?*" asked Luke.

"You!" His face broke into an almost tearful smile. "I had no idea, Luke, honestly. You're a genius. An out-and-out solid-gold star. If I hadn't seen it for myself I would never have believed it. You've *got* to use this gift!"

"So he's on for Sunday then?" Benny said. And Luke could hear him grinning.

Rodney looked back at him, his eyes wide behind his glasses. "I can promise you nothing. Luke's mum is a law unto herself. But on this you have my word – I will use every argument I can think of to persuade her to let him play."

"Magic!" cried Benny.

"Magic!" chorused the players who had all been listening in as well.

"Yes," agreed Rodney, glancing back up at the black redstarts and then at Luke. "I think that's exactly the right word for what I've seen here this morning."

20

Benny Webb drove Luke and Rodney home after training. Luke sat in the back where the day's papers were spread out on the seat. The *Times*, *Sun* and *Express* all had features on him – "Master Green's Masterclass", "Short Pants, Big Prospects", "The Kid Who Makes Michael Owen Look Like A Pensioner". Each one drooled over the chances of him playing on live TV against Villa the next afternoon. Each one also carried the same comment from Luke's "sole agent and close personal friend", Neil Veal: *"No one can yet say if Luke will play and none of you lot can ask him. All access to Luke Green is strictly through me. If anyone so much as whistles at him I'll sue the shin-pads off them"*.

"Boss," asked Luke, as Benny stopped at the corner of their road, "Do you know this bloke Veal? He's telling everyone he's my agent."

"Neil Veal?" Benny sighed into his rear-view mirror. "What can I tell you? Total sleazebucket.

Unacceptable face of modern football. The Fisticuff Five were all on his books. So's Madman. And Chrissie Pick now. He's pushin' him as The Boy With The Biggest Hair In The Nationwide League. He reckons he can get him shampoo ads. I'll say this, though: he's doing us a favour by keeping the media away from your house. Your mum wouldn't be too pleased with twenty reporters shouting through the letter-box, would she? And he *is* on the case round the clock, you have to give him that. Look, he's behind us now."

Luke and Rodney twisted round to see – through a BMW windscreen – a pair of Rayban shades and a glint of golden fangs. "*Lunch?*" Agent Veal was mouthing.

"Come on Luke," said Rodney, "let's go and tackle your mum. I've got a feeling fate is on our side now. I think you're destined to play."

"Triffic," said Benny. "Look, I'll hover out here, and Luke – you can give me a thumbs-up from the bedroom window when you've pulled it off, right?"

"Right, Boss." And with that, Luke scampered after Rodney into the house.

Nan and Grandpa were sitting at the kitchen table which was already laid for lunch. Luke's mum stood fussing by the cooker. It didn't smell great. Pasta with meat sauce, from the look of the browny-red splashes on the wall by the bubbling saucepan. But she was clutching the *Penzance* mug, and the cooking-sherry bottle looked a lot emptier. That should have made her more mellow.

Rodney calmly took up a position by the washing machine and kicked off right away. He didn't even take off his puffer jacket or wipe away the bird mess.

"My dear, I've been giving this a great deal of thought over the past couple of days, so please hear me out. I sense that we may have been a little too quick to punish Luke with regard to his football. He lied to us and that is wrong. He went against your wishes – *our* wishes – and that was not obedient. But the bottom line is this: he only wants to play a game. And, quite obviously he is very *good* at that game. Brilliant, in fact. He has the kind of talent that could be called ... God-given. And is it not wrong – of *us* – to stop him from using it?"

He paused to assess the impact he was having. It was good. Amazingly good. Luke could hardly believe it. His mum was looking at Rodney with a warm half-smile, as if he had suddenly made the scales fall from her eyes.

"When a person has ability of this kind," he went on, "is it not our *duty* to do everything in our power to nurture it, develop it, encourage it...?"

"I have to agree," Grandpa joined in at just the right moment. Luke had known he could depend on Grandpa – he only hoped the old boy didn't punch or squeeze him too hard when they celebrated their triumph any moment now. "I know you can't stand football, love, but it's still the noblest game on earth under all this trashy razzmatazz today. It brings out the best in a lad – courage, determination, putting the team before himself..."

"It can turn a boy into a man," Nan piped up surprisingly, then got flustered and went back to her cup of coffee. But Luke's mum looked at her with a wider smile, and slowly nodded her head as Rodney resumed:

"So you see, dear, I *do* think we over-reacted last week – quite understandably – when we learned about the Hartlepool affair. But now that the dust has settled, we can look to the future: a surely glorious future – if you will let Luke play."

Luke's mum set down her mug, still smiling, still nodding, but looking at the floor now. The silence in the kitchen thickened as Luke, Rodney, Nan and Grandpa all held their breath. Outside, heavy rain began to drum against the windows. "You asked me to hear you out," she said to Rodney – and Luke's stomach flipped as he heard the first faint buzz. "So have you finished now?" The buzz became a hum –

louder, harsher. "Because if you have, I've got just one word to say to you all..."

Humm Crack Pop Fizz. The air was filled by the same kind of racket that went before – and during – an announcement over the Ash Acre tannoy system. Knowing what came next Luke dived headlong out of the room, leaving Nan, Grandpa and Rodney to survive it on their own: *"NNNNOOOO-AAAARRRRGGGGHHHHHH!"*

It powered up the stairs behind Luke like a gale force wind that had just banged its thumb with a hammer. Again it surged up as he raced to his own bedroom window: *"NEVAAAARRRRGGGGGGGHHHHH..."* Wildly Luke shook his head at Benny Webb, but since his car window was wound down he could probably hear Luke's mum's considered opinion for himself. Neil Veal too, because now he was leaning, in the heavy rain, against Benny's bonnet. Then as doors started to slam downstairs, Benny tried to say something back: pointing at Luke and mouthing one word over and over. Luke had no idea what it was.

"I'm too upset to eat!" Luke's mum screamed from the hall. *"I'm going out to the ornamental gardens to get away from this madhouse!"* The front door banged shut, Benny Webb accelerated away (with his beard) for fear of being spotted, leaving Agent Veal with the task of getting the Boss's message across.

Pointing up and miming the mysterious word, he walked closer, along the front of the house. He was hidden from Luke's mum by the high hedge as she stomped down the pathway but – Luke could clearly see – they were heading towards each other on a straight collision course.

And a collision there was. Just as they were about to converge on the pavement, Luke's mum swung up her rolled umbrella in front of her and ferociously shot it open. The blunt metal point cannoned into Agent Veal, driving him backwards and sideways, clutching at his throat, until he toppled into the holly hedge and out of sight. Luke's mum felt something, but when she looked, there was no one there – so she marched off up the street to the gardens.

In a flash Luke was down the stairs and out of the house. Agent Veal was flapping at the prickly leaves, trying to get to his feet. But when he looked up and saw Luke he forced a smile. "Minor mishap," he croaked. "What Benny was saying was 'sub'. He'll still name you as a sub tomorrow – just in case."

Luke shook his head as the agent finally stood and backed towards his BMW.

"Must dash now," he rasped, holding his throat with one hand and pointing at it with the other. "But hey, let's do..." he eyed his Rolex, "...afternoon tea?"

Again Luke shook his head, then slouched back through the rain into the house. So much for phase three of his plan. This was curtains for the shortest career in football history. Two days before, he had thought it was all over. It was now.

21

On Sunday morning Luke's grandparents took him to church. During the service the vicar asked everyone to offer up their own private prayers in silence. Both Nan and Grandpa put a comforting hand on Luke's back. They knew what he was asking God for. They probably also guessed that God still had his earplugs in after yesterday's hair-raising outburst from Luke's mum.

On the way home, big coaches full of people wearing claret and blue were already passing. Villa fans on their way up to Ash Acre. Again, Luke's grandparents silently touched him on either shoulder. Back at the house, Rodney was tiptoeing down the stairs in a pink pinny – and an even less appetizing smell than usual was wafting out of the kitchen.

"She's still in bed," Rodney whispered. "All that arguing yesterday really took it out of her." All *what* arguing? thought Luke. She was the only one saying anything. Or screaming it. "I'm afraid she won't be up to a trip to the garden centre this afternoon," he said, looking apologetically at Nan and Grandpa. "And she asked me to make lunch." Then he looked apologetically at them all.

"Oh well," said Grandpa. "At least we can watch the Villa game on TV now."

"Er – I don't think that's a very good idea," Rodney said quickly, his eyes popping with panic behind his glasses. "She's really – um – very keen *indeed* that no football should ever be watched under this house's roof."

"There, there, love," said Nan, patting his arm. "We won't get you into any more trouble. You've tried your best. This is a rotten old business though."

So too was Rodney's lunch. But even though the roast chicken tasted like damp cardboard and the rice pudding was a suspicious purple colour, that wasn't why Luke hardly ate a mouthful. They were eating at the "special occasion" sitting-room table, and Luke was looking straight out of the window. Minute by minute, more and more soldiers from Benny Webb's blue-and-white army were marching past on their way to the ground. Luke would have given up eating Sunday lunch for the rest of the year just to be with them. And his dad and Cool Frederick were probably already in their seats, soaking up the fantastic pre-match atmosphere, trying to decipher the announcements.

"Look at them: brain-dead," rumbled his mum, who was down in her dressing gown for the meal. Then her face darkened. "But it's not a Saturday, is it?"

Nan, Grandpa, Luke and Rodney all just shrugged. She obviously didn't realize that the Cup-tie had been put back a day to be televised live.

The food combined with the sight of the fans then made her headache worse than before. So while Luke and Rodney washed up she went back to bed. After that, Luke went to his room. And to show solidarity with his team, he put on his mascot kit under the clothes he had worn to church. On this biggest of all big days, it seemed the least he could do. But from his bedroom he could clearly hear the chanting and roaring from Ash Acre.

**"Castle Al-bee-yon. Castle Al-bee-yon.
We'll Support You Evermore!"**
He even heard the piercing whistle that started the match. It was too much for him to bear.

He plodded downstairs and into the back garden. For a few minutes he played keepy-uppy with a tennis ball but still he could hear the great crashing waves of the crowd's noise. You could have heard it all over town. It was a full house, an all-ticket sell-out. 13,500 mad-keen fans packed to the rafters. Or, in the case of the main stand, to the black redstart nest.

Seeing the door at the back of the garage ajar, Luke went inside. So much junk was piled up in there that the Escort had to be parked on the drive. Luke flicked on the light and right away his eye was drawn to it: Rodney's ancient little black-and-white TV that only gave a watchable picture on one channel. Carefully he pulled it down from where it was balancing on a rolled-up carpet, straightened the coat-hanger aerial, plugged it into the socket and switched it on.

Nothing happened. The thing was as dead as Darren Anderton's chances of playing five games without getting injured. Then an entirely new kind of bedlam ballooned up from Ash Acre. More like an outraged howl than a roar, followed by a ghostly, breathy *Ahhhhhh*ing sound – as if 13,500 people had all just been stung by a gigantic nettle.

It made Luke jump up, and as he did so his arm knocked the side of the TV set, bringing it back to life. The din that Luke heard outside the garage was now coming – in a scratchy, crackly form – from the TV too. It only gave you one channel but that channel was BBC1. And that was Albion versus Villa!

Slowly the fuzzy black-and-white picture came up on screen. Watching the World Cup

Final in 1966 must have been like this, Luke thought. But that wasn't England goalie Gordon Banks lying stretched out in the penalty area – it was Madman Mort. And that wasn't Germany's Franz Beckenbauer heaped across him, it was Villa front man Dion Dublin.

"...That really was a very nasty clash, wasn't it, Trevor?" John Motson was saying. "I fear that both Mort and Dublin will be taking no further part in this absorbing and so far finely-balanced Cup-tie. But it was a rather puzzling incident, wasn't it? Dublin was clean through on goal, Mort dashed out..."

"Yeees," Trevor Brooking continued. "If we look at the slow motion here, the oncoming keeper seems to be trying to pull up his own jersey. Can't think why, John. Then Big Dion appears to stumble forward – I mean, er, it was nobody's fault in partic'lar – and as a result they collide at full speed..."

"Well, the stretchers are on and indeed Mort and Dublin will go off. Both sides are warming up substitutes – and already Albion skipper Stuart Mann has pulled on a goalie's jersey, since the Third Division club has only one keeper on its books. *And what's this, Trevor!*" Luke heard another mighty moan mushroom up outside. "*The referee is pointing to the penalty spot!* Even though Mort has not been sent off he is deemed to have fouled Dublin and the Albion players are furious! They're surrounding the referee but he's waving them away."

"And we have an interesting situation here, John, with Dublin – Villa's usual penalty-taker – now off the pitch. Mann has gone between the posts, and he'll have the job of stopping the shot. But it's not yet clear who he'll have to face. The Villa players seem to be having a bit of a debate about it."

"That's right, Trevor. With twenty-eight minutes of this third round FA Cup-tie gone, and with plucky Castle Albion of the Nationwide Third Division holding Aston Villa nil-nil, a hotly-disputed penalty for the visitors will be taken by..."

Luke then heard a colossal hoot of relieved laughter.

"...*Gareth Southgate!*"

22

Luke peered closer at the screen, curling up his toes in his trainers. "Come on Gaffer," he mumbled through gritted teeth. "You can save this."

"Well, would you believe it, Trevor?" John Motson shouted above the crowd's barrage of jeers and whistles. "Gareth Southgate, who will always be remembered for that penalty shoot-out miss for England in the semi-finals of Euro '96, is going to take the responsibility again here at Ash Acre!"

"He's a brave man, <u>John</u>," replied Trevor Brooking. "But he hasn't got a regular goalkeeper to beat now and he must fancy his chances."

The camera closed in on Southgate's face as he got ready to take his run-up. Just like on that night in Euro '96, Luke couldn't bring himself to look. "Miss, miss, *miss*..." he hissed, screwing up his eyes and his fists.

"So here comes Southgate and – *Oh I say!* – he's hit it straight at Stuart Mann!"

There was a sky-shaking cheer. Luke's eyes blinked open. "But the ball has spun up into the air. Southgate follows up!" Luke's eyes shut again. "And it's a simple task for him to nod it into the empty net with the substitute goal-keeper stranded!"

The noise outside the garage died. From the screen came the tinny chirrup of the travelling Villa fans' celebrations. As John Motson went through the goal again in slo-mo, Luke's head slumped forward. Then he felt a strong hand gripping his right shoulder, followed by another on his left.

He froze, trying to work out if the hands were his mum's. Was she about to press him to the garage floor to take a penalty kick of her own with his head? But the hands belonged to two different people. Their owners let go and came up on either side of him.

"Tough luck, lad," said Luke's Grandpa, looking closer at the old TV as Ruel Bibbo kicked off to restart the match.

"Madman would have saved it," snorted Rodney, still in his pink pinny. Luke glanced at him, amazed that he knew who the regular Albion keeper was, let alone his nickname. He and Grandpa were glued to the screen. (Technically, after all, they weren't watching football under the *house*'s roof.)

"W-Where's mum?" Luke asked.

113

"Your nan's gone to sit with her," said Grandpa. "She'll keep her occupied. How long have we got till half-time? Fifteen minutes? There's time yet."

But in all honesty Albion didn't look remotely like equalizing in the next phase of play. Passes went astray. Ruel started to limp. Chopper Foggon seemed to be fighting with Dennis Meldrum over who should mark Stan Collymore.

"That penalty decision seems to have taken the wind out of Castle Albion's sails somewhat," said John Motson. "They've had to reorganize in the light of the unfortunate injury to goalkeeper Mort. And I had been wondering, Trevor, whether manager Benny Webb might have sent on the rising young star Luke Green in Mort's place. He's been named among the substitutes, but as far as I can make out from here, he isn't actually sitting on the bench."

"No, John," agreed Trevor B. "I haven't been able to spot the young lad myself. And I must admit that I'd been hoping he would at least get a run-out today – especially as Chrissie Pick now seems to be struggling with the injury he picked up in the midweek match at Hartlepool. As I understand it, Green brings a whole new dimension to Albion's play down the right side – which is precisely where they're falling short at present."

"By heck, this makes me *mad*!" breathed Grandpa, and for a moment Luke was afraid he might punch the TV set in frustration. "That game's there for the winning. And the lad who could win it is stuck in here watching telly!"

Rodney said nothing. But when Luke glanced his way again, his face seemed to have gone a funny colour. A bit like a Villa shirt in fact: mainly claret with patches of blue around his bulging eyes and tightly-pursed lips.

Back on the pitch, Villa's midfield were starting to run Albion ragged. Two or three minutes at a time went by when no home player got a sniff of the ball. The crowd too was in a state of shock. It was utterly silent outside now. Then after a slick six-man passing move, Villa's Ian Taylor slung in a wickedly curving cross from the left and Ugo Ehiogu, up from the back, flashed a header just over the bar.

"Villa's tails are really up," Mottie observed. "Albion will do well to hang on until half-time without going another goal behind. Then they can perhaps have another look at their game-plan."

"And although we've said it before," Trevor B added, "I can't help thinking the boy Green should figure in the second half. Without him, it's hard to see where a goal's going to come from. I mean, er, as things stand, the service to

Bibbo and Davey just isn't good enough. Green could make all the difference."

"And doubtless," Mottie concluded, " he'd be welcomed as a breath of fresh air by millions of BBC viewers eager to take a look at the youngest-ever player in FA Cup history."

"Right!" boomed Rodney, clamping his hand down on Luke's shoulder again. "That's *it*! Come with me to the Escort. And Grandpa: if anyone asks, Luke and I have gone to take a look at a nest of black redstarts." He stalked out.

Thrilled, Luke turned to follow. "About time too," said Grandpa. "All the best, lad. Show 'em what this game's all about. Oh, but what about your kit?"

In true Madman style, a grinning Luke paused to tug up his Sunday-best pullover. His grandpa winked when he saw the proud blue-and-white hoops underneath.

"This is a victory for football," Luke heard Grandpa say as he rushed out. On third round day anything could happen – *and it had*!

23

In the back of the car Luke struggled out of his jumper and trousers while the Escort clattered through the empty streets. Rodney hadn't even paused to untie the pinny. And his face had turned an even funnier colour (like one of Man U's galaxy of away kits – the blackish one that looks like a ref's outfit). But Luke knew why that was. His stepdad was taking a huge risk here. He felt ill himself just thinking about what his mum would do if she found out.

"I'm really grateful for this," Luke said as they turned into the players' and officials' car park, where there wasn't a single empty space.

Before Rodney could reply, a yellow-jacketed steward came puffing up. The same guy who had tried to move Luke's bike on his mascot day. "Oi," he yelled. "You can't leave that there! You're blocking two of the directors' cars. And anyway, this is for players and officials only."

Rodney jumped from the car and squared up to him, thrusting out his chest in the pink pinny.

"Do you *want* to stay in the Cup?" he asked, as Luke got out too and Rodney pointed his way. "Because without *him*, you won't."

"Ah right, yes, that's different," jabbered the steward, stepping aside to let them both dash past. "Your car's safe here, sir. *And do it for us, Luke!*"

There was a short hold-up at the entrance before Luke and Rodney were waved through. Except at the Villa end, the atmosphere in the ground was deathly. Half-time was nearly over and the tannoy system had broken down completely so there was no music. Even the burger stink seemed fainter than usual.

Luke and Rodney knew where to head for. Down in the warren of offices and lounges, startled-looking staff stood back to let them rush on towards the dressing rooms. Benny Webb's voice boomed out from behind the scuffed blue door marked Home Team. Luke heard every word as he raced towards it:

"You've got to get yourselves *organized*... Use your *brains*... *Think* your way past the opposition... Play *smart* football – can't you?"

Luke came to the door, then paused. Now Gaffer Mann's voice rang out: "That's all very well, Boss. But without the kid, we're just not smart *enough*."

"Without what kid?" asked Rodney, flinging back the door to reveal Luke.

"*It's the Studless Sensation!*" Every single person in the dressing room jumped up from the benches. Even Madman managed a little hop, in spite of his injury. Then Carl Davey hurled his pineapple for Craig Edwards to catch, bent over, and received it back with terrifying force on his bottom.

"*Now* we're in business," grinned Benny Webb, rubbing his hands together. "Chrissie," he shouted as the uproar continued, "I'm taking you off to give that leg a rest. Luke – you're on. Right midfield." The bell clanged summoning the players up from the belly of the stadium for the second forty-five minutes. "It's a game of two halves, lads!" Benny bellowed as they all barged towards the door. "That Premier League bunch had the first one. This one's ours!"

Luke was the last Albion player out of the tunnel. When the announcer spotted him, he desperately tried to tell the crowd: "*Castle Albion start the second half with LUKE GREEN replacing Chrissie Pick!*" But after the first two crackly words his voice spluttered into silence again.

Benny Webb yelled up at him in his box next to Mottie and Trevor's gantry: "Get your act together, will you – we want that thing working! There'll be lots more to crow about this half!"

It didn't matter, though. On three sides of the ground the Albion faithful saw the thrilling truth for themselves. And the redstarts must have had the fright of their lives when a deafening new chorus threatened to lift off the old stand roof:

"ONE Lukey Green!
There's Only ONE Lukey Green...!"

Luke grinned and felt like waving. He could see a TV camera just under the South Side clock pointing at him. Millions of armchair fans all over Britain (who had probably had a far better lunch than him) were now staring at *his* face! His grin grew broader still and he couldn't resist mouthing: *Hi, Grandpa*, while thanking his lucky stars he was too far away for Grandpa to whack him with pride.

Villa manager John Gregory trotted out of the tunnel behind Luke and ruffled his hair as he passed. Luke's first instinct was to race after him and ask for his autograph. But that could wait. Now he had a job to do.

The fans were still screaming his name as if their lives depended on it:

"Come on, Lu-uke. Come on Lu-uke..."

Lining up behind Carl Davey, wide on the right of midfield, Luke hoped his mum was fast asleep. If she heard thousands of her least favourite people in the world chanting her son's name, she would probably throw open the window and drown them all out with a specially turbo-charged *Aaarrrgggghhhhh!* of her own.

The ref checked with his two assistants and blew his whistle. The crowd cranked up the volume higher still. This is it, thought Luke. Game on.

24

Straight from the kick-off Albion went for it. With the floodlights now on, Luke pushed up on the Villa back four as Dennis Meldrum slid a ball inside the full-back for Ruel to run on to. Not limping now, Ruel took it up to the edge of the area and dummied a pass back to the over-lapping Dennis. Then with hardly any backlift – and without even looking at the goal – he chipped a lovely shot over keeper Michael Oakes' head towards the top far corner of the net.

"It's there!" Albion's Army hollered in amazement. And even Luke threw up his arms in jubilation, almost skidding in his trainers. But the Villa goalie had kept so many clean sheets in recent weeks, he could have started a laundry – and he wasn't about to lose his record at Ash Acre. Arching his back, he propelled himself up until he was almost horizontal. Then to the Albion fans' groans he flipped the ball over the bar with one outstretched arm.

Luke took the resulting corner himself – a floater that hung for Ruel to leap for, although on this occasion Ugo Ehiogu got in first. But Luke noticed that as soon as he'd kicked the ball, the Villa defenders stepped up – just a little way – and left the near post slightly unguarded. *Play SMART football*, he remembered Benny Webb pleading. OK Boss, he thought. Next time...

First he had to backtrack as Villa turned defence into attack. The way these guys fizzed passes around at speed was a joy to see. Luke half-wished he was watching it on TV, so that he could appreciate it properly and then hear Alan Hansen picking holes in it afterwards. *Concentrate!* he told himself, finally intercepting a short ball. He swivelled round and sent a lovely forty-yard pass across to Dennis Meldrum who was still chugging back from the corner. Unfortunately Dennis wasn't expecting it and the ball ran under his foot into touch.

That didn't please Chopper. For the next few minutes he gave the poor guy a right roasting. Chopper was well hyped up for this game. Soon he was abusing the whole Albion team as they fought off a flurry of laser-quick Villa attacks: "We're sitting back! We gotta get at 'em! Get on the offensive. Offensive! OFFENSIVE!" (And if anyone knew the meaning of *that* word, it was him.)

Benny Webb was now out on the cinder track, tugging at his beard and bawling instructions that no one could possibly hear. Even when Luke ran within ten yards of him to take a throw-in, he could barely decipher a word. For all the sense he made, he could still have been doing his mime outside Luke's house the day before – or trying to teach the crowd about the Spanish Armadillo. But after sending a crossfield ball to Half-Fat Milkes, Luke noticed a flash of pink in the Albion dug-out. Rodney! In amongst the subs. In his pinny! As their eyes met, Luke laughed. Then Rodney raised a fist and shouted something fiercely supportive like "*We can have these!*" But again no words sounded at all.

Slowly the tide began to turn in Albion's favour. Fifty-fifty balls started to go their way. Villa couldn't seem to get out of their own half. Luke enjoyed more and more possession – playing the ball short, long, into space, straight to feet. And not once did he fall on his backside. Seeing that he was running the show, Villa moved up Alan Wright to mark him man-for-man. "Stick with the kid!" Southgate kept shouting. "Shut down that kid!"

And for a short spell Wright did just that. Everywhere Luke went, the classy Premier League defender got there a split second earlier. It was mightily frustrating but there was nothing Luke could do. "Nut him when he's not looking!" Chopper Foggon growled after one tackle, but he ignored that.

Then Luke's moment came. Ruel tried another chip – not quite so fine as before but Oakes still had to push it round his post. Corner. And even Alan Wright had to stand ten yards away when Luke went over to take it. Ten yards was all Luke needed. Ten yards – and the crack of space that opened up between Steve Watson and the near post when Luke pretended to take the kick but then let his foot hang. As soon as he saw the gap he swung his shot directly into the net. *It was there!* No wind-assisted fluke like that soft goal at Hartlepool. This was the Gospel according to Benny Webb – *smart* football!

The crowd exploded, seeming to lift Luke off his feet even before his team-mates reached him in the corner and lifted him all over again. As they carried him back to the halfway line the tannoy burst into life but only for the duration of *"Albion's equalizing goal was – burp – scored by – pishhhh – LUKE GR..."*

The next passage of play went by in a daze, and not just for Luke. Stung into action, Villa seemed to find another gear. Luke realized then how true it is when people say a team is at its weakest just after scoring a goal. None of the Albion's players could get a look-in. Three times in five minutes the defence was cut to shreds.

Twice Gaffer Mann had to make heroic last-ditch saves. The third time, Dennis Meldrum cleared from under the bar with an overhead kick. That, at least, got Chopper off his back for a while. But still he gasped on: "Offensive...! Offensive...! Offensive...! *Offensive!*"

Luke glanced up at the South Side clock. Six minutes left. Villa continued to surge forward. They weren't interested in taking Albion back to Villa Park for a replay. They had come here to win at the first time of asking. And when they won a corner, everyone but Southgate, Taylor and Wright went up for it. Luke began to run back too, to help to defend. But then for the first time he heard Benny Webb's voice from the touchline. "No! No! You stay up front, son. Stay up with Ruel and give us an option!" Luke stopped in his tracks and jogged back to the halfway line to watch the corner float in.

It skimmed into the box, deceiving two Albion men with its wicked curve, but Gaffer Mann was equal to it. He came off his line and – because he was unsure if he could catch it – he punched that ball in much the same way that everyone else in the team had been wanting to punch Chopper Foggon all afternoon.

It sailed out of the area, over to the right wing where Luke was waiting. He ran back to collect it. Wright, as ever, was directly behind. But instead of trying to turn and beat him, Luke flicked the ball inside to Ruel, then spun around and raced away to receive the return. Ruel read it like the *Beano*. He played a perfect one-two, and suddenly Luke was in oceans of space, with Wright in his slipstream and only Southgate and Taylor between him and the keeper.

Luke raced forward. "Get the kid! Get the kid!" Southgate was shouting. And as Ruel streaked into the box like a player half his age, Taylor edged across to challenge Luke. The Studless Sensation saw what he had to do. Before Taylor could get any closer, he whipped in a fabulous near-post cross *behind* Southgate and on to the head of whippet-like Ruel. The big man had to score!

25

Ruel met it firm and true. It was just like the day when Luke had been mascot, firing in those three crosses which the striker had slotted home in the pre-match kick around. But this was no kick around. This was Round Three of the FA Cup.

The keeper flung himself to his left to beat out the ball just before it crossed the line. The crowd's "Oooohhhh...!" seemed to gush right through Luke. But then he saw that the ball wasn't going out for a corner. Taylor saw it a fraction of a second later. Luke hurtled past him, used his flat-bottomed trainers to skid forward faster, and hooked the ball back into the six-yard box from the byline.

This time it looped to the far post, again beyond Southgate, and Ruel rose majestically to direct his header down to the scrambling keeper's right. "Aaaahhhhh...!" the crazed Albion thousands bayed now, as the astoundingly athletic netminder somehow scooped the ball up and away from his line.

It flew across the box between Southgate and the inrushing Luke. The England man started to come for it. Then he hesitated for fear of leaving Ruel unmarked, which let Luke get his head to it first. With his keeper still on the deck, Gareth Southgate hurled himself through the air to block Luke's header at goal. But Smart Luke Green didn't aim at the goal. As Southgate sailed across in front of him, he laid back a cushioned little header to the waiting Ruel – who trapped it, looked up with glee, and smashed it into the roof of the net.

"GOOOOOOAAAAAAAAAALLLLLLLLLL!" as the Brazilian commentators say. "*And Albion's second goal ... plink ... phut...*" was as far as the Ash Acre announcer got. But even if the tannoy hadn't packed up again, no one would have heard. There was more noise in the ground than Wembley Stadium jam-packed with Zeppelin impersonators. Half the Albion team mobbed Ruel, the other half dived on Luke. Then everyone changed places and both scorer and passer had to go through it all again.

Meanwhile Benny Webb was doing a brilliant impression of a windmill in front of the dug-out. Neither Luke nor any of his team-mates knew what he meant. He probably didn't know himself. Behind him on the cinder track Rodney was doing a mad little war-dance in his pinny. (*Phoenicurus ochruros*, eat your hearts out!)

Even the man who was trying to reconnect the tannoy wires swung round and round on his ladder waving his arm.

But Villa weren't going to lie down and die. This was a club that had *won* the FA Cup seven times. They bombarded the Albion area with crosses and their big men from the back set up camp in the six-yard box. Every time Stuart Mann rose to fist the ball away, a Villa boot reached it first and thumped it back in – until Luke dropped a little deeper and nicked it away from Hendrie. Glancing up, he saw a vast stretch of space between himself and the Villa corner flag. "Go for the flag, you little runt!" Chopper bawled from behind him. "Get it in the corner and waste the last few seconds!"

Luke set off as the Villa midfielders came swarming back. But he didn't head for the corner. The element of surprise. He'd seen a smarter option: Carl Davey bombing up through the middle and still onside. Luke took aim and rolled the sweetest little ball through the backpedalling Villans into Carl's path.

From thirty-five yards the Pineapple Poacher hit a perfect peach. Bending like a top-speed banana, it was in the net before the keeper could move – and that was the cherry on Albion's cake. Carl took off on a victory sprint – about to point to his bottom but then deciding against it – when the ref blew up for full time.

Then, as the crowd went beserk, something bizarre happened. The tannoy started to work. Every word blared out as clear as a bell.

"*So Carl Davey wraps it up for the underdogs with a last-minute killer goal!*" But this wasn't the announcer's voice. This was a feverishly excited John Motson! The wires had got crossed and now the TV commentary was booming all around Ash Acre.

"*And I don't know about you, Trevor,*" Mottie raved on, "*but I certainly can't remember seeing a more masterful midfield display than the one given to us today by Luke Green – who surely has to be everybody's choice as man-of-the-match. Or – heh, heh – should that be YOUNG-man-of-the-match!*"

Contact was lost again before Trevor Brooking could reply. But the fans were already filling the floodlit winter skies with their own appreciation:

"We Love You Lukey – Oh Yes We Do!
We Love You Lukey – Oh YESSSS We Do!"

The pitch had been invaded from three sides, but the police and stewards made a corridor for the players to run down in safety. "Good game, son," the shell-shocked John Gregory said as Luke dashed past him into the arms of first Benny Webb, and then an absolutely rampant Rodney.

131

"*We had 'em! We had 'em! We had 'em!*" was all his hoarse stepdad could keep on yelling.

"You did us proud, son," Benny grinned. "Smart, smart, smart!"

"Cheers, Boss," said Luke, his words swallowed by the uproar. He was craning his neck to catch a sight of his dad. His seat was just behind the dug-out but Luke couldn't see him. Forcing his way up into the stand, he suddenly came face-to-face with Cool Frederick who was standing alone in the gangway above an exit. "Respect," Frederick said warmly from under his Walkman as he high-fived his mate.

"But where's my dad?" Luke hollered back.

Just then, a shouting match broke out beneath them in the exit. "Luke! Luke! Luke!" one man was jabbering. "No way, I'm afraid. No way," another spat back. Luke looked down to see his dad trying to come *up* the steps from the street. And Agent Veal was blocking not just him, but Gary Lineker too, who was trying to get to Luke with his mike for a post-match interview. "My client is talking to no one," he was saying. "All enquiries go through me."

"Your *client*!" Luke's dad laughed, wrestling with him. "But that's my *boy*!"

"Dad! Dad!" Luke called down. "Why aren't you up here?"

"I was locked out!" he explained at the top of his voice. "They sold my ticket twice over again! I never saw a minute. But I heard it Luke! Oh baby, *I heard*!"

"You're his *dad*?" Agent Veal asked, letting the guitarist go and smoothing down his floral satin jacket. "Well, hey." He put an arm round his shoulder and led him away towards the tea bar. "Let's do Bovril – and talk some numbers."

Then a hand gripped Luke's and pulled him back down towards the pitch. It was Rodney – and he looked horribly agitated. "I hate to drag you away," he said, "but your mum will expect me to have tea on the table any minute. We've got to go. We can't let her get suspicious, can we?"

But even as he spoke they were caught up in a mad charge of players and officials – and found themselves being pushed down the tunnel. Every person they passed clapped Luke on the back or shook his hand. One huge steward munching a ghastly-burger planted a big ketchupy kiss on the top of his head.

Moments later they reached the home dressing-room. Anyone connected with the club for the past fifty years seemed to be inside – dancing and shouting and shooting champagne corks.

"Here, Luke!" Carl Davey bellowed, popping his head round a door up ahead that had *Bath* written on it. "Get in here! We're gonna listen to the Fourth Round draw! Benny's got a radio!"

Luke looked at the panic-stricken Rodney and couldn't help grinning. "That pinny," he laughed. "You've had it on all afternoon."

"Don't knock it," Rodney shouted over the tumult after yet another glance at his watch. "I wore it today and you won, didn't you? You haven't seen the last of it either. I'm going to wear it for every single Cup game till you get knocked out."

"Good thinking!" roared Madman Mort, hobbling now but still able to sweep Rodney off his feet as he passed – and cart him on through the doorway. "Come on, Studless," yelled the keeper over his shoulder as Rodney pummelled his back. "Get in with us! All for one and one for all!"

Still laughing, Luke followed. He'd never been in here before. He found it pretty odd that clubs still *had* one big bath for all the players. But here, steaming beneath him, was Castle Albion's. Dennis, Narris, Ruel, Craig and Chrissie were already in and only their heads showed above the choppy water.

"*Studless! Studless! Studless!*" they chorused, thrusting up their arms and pointing Luke's way.

"*Studless! Studless!*" Carl, Half-Fat and Gaffer joined in from the side – still in their kit and boots – before giving the second-half hero a great big hug.

"STUDLESS! STUDLESS!" added another voice – louder than all the rest put together. It came from the unearthly throat of Madman Mort – as he rose like a Loch Ness Monster in full goalie kit from under the water. And drenched, pink-pinnied Rodney was still up there on his shoulder and still pummelling his back!

"OK, shut it, you wonderful ugly lot!" boomed Benny Webb from the corner in his steamed-up sheepskin. He turned up an ancient transistor radio to top volume. "Now let's hear who we're gonna get in the next round!"

Castle Albion's Crazy Cup-Run
Continues With. . .

COME AND HAVE A GO IF YOU THINK YOU'RE COOL ENOUGH!

Benny didn't introduce the newcomer to the rest of the squad. Most of them had met him already. Frederick had travelled up to the Hartlepool game as Luke's guest. Then at a service-station kick around on the way home, he had shown so much skill that Benny had invited him for a trial. This, at last, was it.

The manager had promised a stiff session and he wasn't kidding. Since this was the first time they had trained on grass for two weeks, Benny made sure everyone remembered what it tasted like: hundreds of press-ups, dozens of wheelbarrow races, lots of sheer flat-out gasping for breath. "Can't we practise diving in the penalty area now?" panted midfielder Michael "Half-Fat" Milkes.

"You keep working, Milkesey, and get some of that weight off," Benny shouted back. "I don't know about 'Half Fat'. From where I'm standing you look more like Full Fat with Extra Cream."

"Oh do behave, Boss," Dennis Meldrum

pleaded. "Can't we do something with a *ball*? We're gonna forget what it looks like, come Saturday."

"OK then, Dennis, just for you." The manager tossed a ball into the full-back's arms. "Run round the pitch ten times holding that in front of you."

But after another fifteen minutes of back-breaking exercises, Benny got everyone together and picked two sides for a practice match – with work experience lads making up the numbers. He put both Luke and Frederick on Team Two. "You, son," he said to Frederick. "Where do you normally play?"

"In a baby bouncer?" sneered a bullet-headed veteran with tree-trunk thighs, standing apart from everyone else, and with his arms folded. Some of the others tittered. It was usually a good idea to titter at this guy's "jokes". If you didn't, and you got him on a bad day, he had ways of *making* you laugh. For this was Chopper Foggon, Albion's leaky defensive stopper (*motto*: It's Good To Talk, But Better To Bite). Frederick smiled straight back at him and nodded. "Sweeper," he told Benny.

"Well, we're playing with a flat back-four now," Benny said. "You'll have to slot in as a twin centre half alongside Gaffer Mann. Give it your best shot."

The game was pretty messy to start with.

Then Luke threaded a ball past Chopper for Half-Fat to run on to. The midfielder shot first time and Madman tipped it away for a corner. Gaffer Mann waved Frederick up for the set piece, which Luke ran across to take. While he was placing the ball he saw Chopper jostling his mate on the goal-line. Just his usual week-in, week-out stuff: an elbow here, a shirt-tug there. Frederick took it all in his stride and as soon as Luke started his run-up, he ghosted out towards him.

Luke understood. They had practised this move over and over in the park. He had to drop his corner just inside the six-yard box. Then Frederick would hook it back over his own head and into the goal. Luke flighted the ball in, but just as Frederick went for it, Chopper clipped his heels. Down went Luke's mate – but, with breathtaking agility, he sprang up again to meet the cross on the volley and caress it into the net at Madman's near post. One-nil to Team Two.

Chopper didn't look best pleased as Frederick was mobbed and the game restarted. And he didn't get much happier over the next half an hour. His side spent most of the time encamped in Team Two's half, so he couldn't get much chopping in. All he *could* do – along with everyone else – was admire the silky defensive skills of the new schoolboy trialist.

There were no two ways about it, this kid was

tasty. He was shadowing ex-West Brom, Chelsea and Tottenham striker Ruel Bibbo – once one of the first black players to be capped by England. But however many balls were lofted or driven into Team Two's box, Frederick always got there first. By the time Ruel pulled up short with his regular groin-strain and went off for treatment, he hadn't had a single shot.

With fewer defensive duties, Frederick began to link smoothly with Luke in midfield. The two boys' interpassing was different class. In one zigzagging move they cut Team One to shreds – and put Half-Fat clean through on goal again. Chopper wasn't having any of that. Puffing along in the midfielder's wake, he shot out a leg and scythed him down. Penalty.

Craig Edwards stepped up. He hit the kick hard and well to Madman's left. But the keeper spread himself brilliantly and fisted it away. Then he raced to the North Stand to receive fanatical acclaim from all the empty seats. Benny had seen enough. He blew the final whistle: "Last one in the bath likes Chelsea!"

As the players trooped off, no one passed Frederick and Luke without a good-natured wind-up: "You won't be too bad when you grow up, son." "Where'd you learn those moves – *Blue Peter*?" Only Chopper stomped by in silence. Even his beads of sweat looked stroppy.

Paul Stewart

Football Mad

2-1 up in the inter-school cup final, captain
Gary Connell finds the net … at the wrong end!
Now cup glory rests on a tricky replay…

Football Mad 2

Offside!

The inter-school cup is up for grabs again. But
Craig won't be playing. He's been dropped –
and he's not happy…

Football Mad 3

Hat-trick!

Could it be cup-final number three?
Goalkeeper Danny is in trouble. New team
coach Mr Carlton has really got it in for him…

Creatures

The Series With Bite!

Everyone loves animals. The birds in the trees. The dogs running in the park. That cute little kitten.

But don't get too close. Not until you're sure. Are they ordinary animals – or are they creatures?

1. Once I Caught a Fish Alive
Paul's special new fish is causing problems. He wants to get rid of it, but the fish has other ideas...

2. If You Go Down to the Woods
Alex is having serious problems with the school play costumes. Did that fur coat just move?

3. See How They Run
Jon's next-door neighbour is very weird. In fact, Jon isn't sure that Frankie is completely human...

4. Who's Been Sitting in My Chair?
Rhoda's cat Opal seems to be terrified ... of a chair! But then this chair belongs to a very strange cat...

Look out for these new creatures...

5. Atishoo! Atishoo! All Fall Down!
Chocky the mynah bird is a great school pet. But now he's turning nasty. And you'd better do what he says...

6. Give a Dog a Bone
A statue of a faithful dog sounds really cute. But this dog is faithful unto death. And beyond...

Creatures – you have been warned!

HURRICANE HAMISH

Mark Jefferson

HURRICANE HAMISH
THE CALYPSO CRICKETER

Hurricane Hamish has always been a bit special – ever since he was found washed up on a Caribbean beach wrapped in an MCC towel. He's only twelve, but he can bowl fast. Really fast. So fast he might be about to play for the West Indies...

HURRICANE HAMISH
THE CRICKET WORLD CUP

Hurricane Hamish is back – and now he's in England, determined to help the West Indies win the Cricket World Cup. But England is so cold! The grounds are so wet and slippery that Hurricane can't even stay standing, let alone bowl fast...

"The ideal literary companion for this summer's Carnival of Cricket – the World Cup."
Lord MacLaurin, Chairman of the England and Wales Cricket Board

"Mark Jefferson has scored a real winner with Hurricane Hamish ... this pacey romp of a book."
Christina Hardyment, The Independent

"A novel which, like its hero, has pace and heart."
Nicolette Jones, The Sunday Times